THE LETHAL TARGET

THE MALICHEA QUEST

Also by Jim Eldridge

The Invisible Assassin
The Deadly Game

THE LETHAL TARGET

THE MALICHEA QUEST

JIM ELDRIDGE

BLOOMSBURY
LONDON NEW DELHI NEW YORK SYDNEY

Bloomsbury Publishing, London, New Delhi, New York and Sydney

First published in Great Britain in April 2013 by
Bloomsbury Publishing Plc
50 Bedford Square, London WC1B 3DP

Copyright © Jim Eldridge 2013

A CIP catalogue record for this book is available from the British Library

ISBN 978 1 4088 1721 6

MIX
Paper from
responsible sources
FSC® C020471

Typeset by Hewer Text UK Ltd, Edinburgh
Printed in Great Britain by CPI Group (UK) Ltd, Croydon CR0 4YY

1 3 5 7 9 10 8 6 4 2

www.bloomsbury.com
www.jimeldridge.com

To Lynne, for ever

The scream echoed through the tunnel and into the cellar room. A man, screaming in fear. Then suddenly the scream was cut off.

The two men in the cellar didn't react; they were concentrating on the equipment on a small metal table: a hypodermic needle and a series of glass phials containing some sort of liquid. The cellar was old, the sandstone and brick walls almost black with age. A metal bed frame had been screwed to the floor. No mattress, just the frame, with thick wire acting as crude springs. Iron manacles dangled from the bars at its head and foot.

The door of the cellar opened and two uniformed men entered, their uniforms army khaki, black jackboots on their feet shining dully in the half-light. Between them they held a naked man. A strip of thick grey tape had been fixed across his mouth to stop him screaming any more. The man looked towards the metal bed frame in the centre of the cellar. He tried to pull back, his eyes bulging with fear, sweat pouring down his face, his bare feet kicking out; but the grip of the men who held him was too strong.

'Put him on it,' said one of the watching men in Russian.

The two uniformed men dragged the prisoner towards the bed frame and pushed him down on to the wire springs. One sat on him, stopping him from moving, while the other fixed the manacles to his wrists and ankles. Then they stepped back.

The man on the bed began to buck and twist, pulling desperately at the manacles, his actions tearing open the skin of his wrists and ankles as they rubbed against the iron.

The man in command picked up the hypodermic needle from the table. He inserted it into one of the glass phials through the opening at the top and drew some of the liquid into the syringe.

'Hold him,' he ordered the two uniformed men, again in Russian. They moved to the bed frame and pressed their combined weight down on the struggling prisoner, holding him firmly in place. The man pushed the needle deep into the thigh of the hostage and slowly pushed the plunger down until the syringe was empty. Then he stepped back and nodded to the two men, who instantly released their hold on the prisoner.

The two soldiers retreated to the cellar door, where they stood and waited. All four men kept their eyes on the hostage chained to the bed frame.

One minute passed, then two, then three. Suddenly wisps of smoke began to appear from the pores in the man's skin, tiny at first, then getting denser. The man struggled, his eyes wide in a mixture of pain and fear, his body arching and thrashing. Then a gush of smoke escaped from his nostrils. Smoke was pouring out of the man, through his skin, his scalp, his feet, his arms . . .

There was a sudden silent explosion, intense white flames bursting out through the smoke, coming from inside the man, and the next second the figure on the bed was a heaving mass of fire, the heat and glare making the watching men recoil.

Almost as suddenly as the fire had begun, it stopped, and there was just a cloud of oily smoke, while ashes fell through the bed frame's wire springs to the cellar floor. All that remained of the captive was the hands and feet, still enclosed in the iron manacles, the whites of the bones visible through the scorched flesh.

The other man by the table, who had been silent so far, shook his head.

'The reaction was too slow,' he said in English. 'We need the book.'

'Our people are looking for it as we speak,' replied the other. He looked at the smouldering pile of ashes and burnt bone. 'This one was too big. I believe the excess fat under his skin caused the slow reaction time.' He nodded thoughtfully, then called an order to the men by the door. 'Bring in the young woman!' To the man next to him, he growled: 'Her flesh should burn faster.'

Chapter 1

Jake was worried; very worried. He walked around the supermarket, filling up his trolley with his week's supplies, moving on automatic pilot. All he could think of was Lauren. It had been five days since he'd last spoken to her, and that had been by phone, not even Skype, so he hadn't had the chance to see how she looked. She'd sounded odd. Nervous. He knew she couldn't say why, their conversations were monitored by the intelligence services, but usually they found a way to drop a hint if something was worrying one of them, so they could read between the lines, put together the clues in texts and phone calls. But this last time, no hint, just an awareness in Jake that something was troubling Lauren. And since that last phone call, nothing. No texts, no emails, no phone calls, no letters.

It was at times like this he felt the distance between them: her in New Zealand and him in London.

The previous night, when it was daytime in New Zealand, he'd even phoned the place where she worked, the Antarctic Survey Research Centre in Wellington, in case something had happened to her, a serious accident, and she wasn't able to make contact with him. But the woman he'd spoken to had said Samantha Adams (Lauren's cover name in New Zealand) hadn't been in to work for four days, and they hadn't heard from her, which was very unusual.

They'd been in touch with Lauren's flatmate, a young woman called Kristal, who said that Lauren had told her she was going away for a day or so, and not to worry. So she hadn't. But since the Survey Research Centre had got in touch, Kristal had contacted the local police and hospitals to see if there had been any reports of an unidentified young woman having been in an accident; but there had been nothing.

'We're very worried about her,' the woman told Jake. 'This is so unlike her. If you hear from her, would you ask her to get in touch with us?'

Jake promised he would. Just as he was about to ring off, the woman asked him if Samantha had any Russian connections.

'Russian connections?' Jake frowned.

'It's just that on the last day she was in the office she had a call from someone, and the switchboard operator was fairly sure the person was Russian.'

'A man or a woman?'

'A man.'

A Russian? Jake was puzzled. Lauren had never mentioned knowing any Russians. But then it had been five months since they'd last seen one another. Anything could have happened in that time. What was clear was that Lauren seemed to have vanished suddenly, and without trace . . .

I have to go to New Zealand, decided Jake. Maybe someone had got hold of her and was holding her prisoner.

His mobile beeped to let him know he had a text. He opened it, and read: *L needs your help*, followed by a phone number.

His heart leapt. Lauren! But why wasn't she phoning — why text?

He checked the screen for the number that had called him, but was told it was 'number withheld'. Which didn't make sense, as whoever had texted him had given him a phone number. It was an 01680 area code, and he had no idea where that was.

He tapped out the number. It rang for a few seconds, and then a woman's voice with a soft Scottish accent said: 'Craigmount Guest House.'

'Hi,' said Jake. 'My name's Jake Wells. I had a message to call this number.'

'Oh yes, Mr Wells,' said the woman. 'Miss Cooper told us to expect your call. We've sent you an email

7

with our address and how to get here. Do you know when you'll be arriving?'

'Er . . .' Jake was too taken aback to reply immediately. Arriving? Why? Then he remembered the message: *L needs your help.*

'Where are you?' he asked.

'Not far from Craignure,' said the woman. 'If the email hasn't arrived, just call and we'll send it again.'

'I mean, where are you, specifically?' asked Jake. 'Southern England, northern, Wales . . .'

'The Isle of Mull,' said the woman, sounding a little surprised. 'Scotland.'

'Oh yes, of course,' lied Jake. 'I'm sorry, I was getting confused.'

The Isle of Mull? Jake recalled an obscure press release from his time as a press officer at the Department of Science mentioning Mull. It was one of the Hebridean islands off the west coast of Scotland. How long would it take him to get there?

'I should be arriving sometime tomorrow,' he said, making a guess.

'Check the ferry times from Oban,' said the woman. 'We've included them in the email. Will you be coming by car or as a foot passenger? I ask because we can arrange to meet you if you let us know which ferry you'll be coming on.'

8

'I'll be driving,' said Jake. Then, as an afterthought, he added: 'Is Miss Cooper there? Could I talk to her?'

'I'm afraid she's out at the moment,' said the woman.

'Perhaps you could get her to call me when she comes in,' asked Jake.

'I'm very sorry, Miss Cooper left instructions she can't receive or make phone calls,' said the woman, and Jake noted the genuine note of apology in her voice as she said it.

Why? wondered Jake.

'No problem,' he said.

'In that case, we look forward to seeing you tomorrow,' said the woman.

Jake hung up.

In the two months since he'd been sacked from the department he'd had time on his hands, so he'd learnt to drive. It hadn't been as hard as he'd thought. He didn't yet have a car of his own, but he could hire one. He wondered if it would be better to hire one here in London and drive all the way to Mull, or catch a train and hire one when he got to . . . where was it the woman had said? Oban.

He'd check it out as soon as he got home, once he'd looked at the email.

L needs your help. But the woman he'd spoken to on Mull hadn't sounded as if there was a panic situation. But who was this Miss Cooper?

He looked at the items in his trolley: food, snacks, milk, washing-up liquid. Well, I won't be needing any of these if I'm going to be in Scotland, he thought. He dumped the trolley at the end of an aisle, and headed home. The sooner he was on his way to Mull, the better.

He was relieved to find the email from Craigmount Guest House in his inbox, with details of where the guest house was on the southern part of the island, and links to the ferry operator's timetable of sailings. Within an hour he had his journey north arranged. By tomorrow afternoon he'd be talking to this mysterious Miss Cooper face to face.

He was packing for the trip when his phone beeped. It was a text: *Don't go to Mull.*

Chapter 2

Jake stared at the text.

Don't go to Mull.

Who'd sent it? And why? There was no clue. Whoever had texted him had made sure their own number stayed secret.

It has to be something to do with MI5, reasoned Jake. He knew his phone and his computer were kept under surveillance. That had been the case ever since Lauren had been sent to exile in New Zealand. So they would have been hacking in and learnt about Mull. There was no one else he could think of that would be bothered. It had been a long while since he'd had any contact with Pierce Randall, the dubious but wealthy international law firm, over the hidden books. And they'd already double-crossed him twice, so they were unlikely to be in contact with him. No, it had to be MI5 warning him off. But why?

He looked at the text again.

Don't go to Mull.

Well, the hell with that, thought Jake. The woman I love needs my help; and if that means going to Mull, then there's nothing on earth that's going to stop me going there.

At half past eleven that night, Jake arrived at Euston station by taxi, his overnight bag packed with essentials. He didn't know how long he'd be away for: two days or a month. It didn't matter. There was nothing for him to stay in London for.

At this time of night, the subterranean taxi area was almost deserted, just a few late-night people trying to get home and a couple of taxis at the rank. Jake headed up the stairs towards the ground-level concourse. Two young men wearing hoodies were coming down the stairs. Jake moved to one side to let them pass, but the two men moved with him, blocking his way. At first, Jake couldn't see their faces — their hoods were pulled well forward — but then he realised they also had scarves pulled up under their hoods so that only their eyes were visible.

Trouble! thought Jake.

Jake moved again, to the other side of the stairs, but again the two men moved with him, blocking his way.

OK, thought Jake. I either stay here and fight them, and get beaten up and robbed, and miss my train; or I do a runner.

Jake moved suddenly to his left, sliding under the metal rail that divided the up and the down stairs, and began to run. He wasn't quick enough. Being upstairs from him, the two men had the advantage. They both darted under the handrail and leapt at Jake. Jake swung his overnight bag and hit one of them hard, sending him stumbling back. Seeing that the man was caught off-balance, Jake swung his bag again, this time thumping it with all his might against the side of the man's head. The man fell tumbling down the stairs, with a sickening crunching sound as he bounced down from step to step.

Jake went to swing the bag back to ward off the other attacker, but he was too late; the guy was on him, the fingers of one hand digging into Jake's throat. Jake realised with horror that he had a knife in his other hand.

Frantically, Jake brought his bag up, just as the man swung the knife, and felt the knife blade sink into his bag. But his attacker's fingers on his throat were like an iron claw, closing, strangling . . .

'Oi!'

The shout came from down below.

Suddenly, the man's grip was released, and then he was off running up the stairs. Jake looked down and saw a thickset man hurrying up.

'Are you all right?' asked the man.

'Just about,' said Jake. His voice sounded hoarse from where the man had tried to strangle him.

His rescuer shook his head.

'Muggers!' he said disgustedly. 'More police here, that's the answer! It's all very well them being here in the middle of the day, but it's this time of night those scum operate!' He looked anxiously at Jake. 'You sure you're all right?'

'Yes, thanks.' Jake nodded. 'Though I wouldn't have been if you hadn't come along. Did you see the other one?'

The man frowned.

'The other one?'

'Yes. There were two of them, but I knocked the other one down the stairs with my bag.'

'Good for you!' The man grinned. Then he frowned again. 'But I didn't see anyone else. He must have scarpered when he heard my cab pull up.'

'Well, thanks,' said Jake.

He felt the side of his bag. The knife wasn't there. His attacker must have taken it.

Jake found his seat on the train and settled himself down for the long journey. There had been a sleeping berth available, but it would have meant sharing, and Jake didn't fancy the idea of being trapped in a sleeping compartment with someone he didn't know, who might be a drunk, or deranged, or snore loudly. He'd decided he'd rather spend the night trying to sleep in one of the comfortable seats.

As he sat down, his phone went. Another text: *We warned you. Don't go to Mull.*

A sickening feeling went through him. So those guys hadn't been muggers; it had been a deliberate attack on him. The man had tried to stab him. If Jake hadn't used his bag to stop the knife, he'd be dead!

The attack didn't have the style of an MI5 operation: two hooded youths. But a late-night mugging in London, a stabbing, could be passed off as just another statistic. But why? What was there on Mull that was so important that they were prepared to kill Jake to stop him getting there? And who were *they*?

Chapter 3

Jake didn't get any sleep for the first part of the journey. He spent most of the night watching his phone, waiting for further text messages warning him off, but there were none.

He was also too frightened to go to sleep in case his mystery attackers had put someone on the train. If they could arrange the attack on him at Euston station, they could certainly put someone on the train to follow him, and kill him.

Finally, after what seemed an age, he managed to doze off as tiredness came over him. But even then, it was a fitful sleep, half awake, opening his eyes every few moments. By the time the train pulled into Glasgow Central station just after quarter past seven the next morning, Jake felt exhausted.

But soon, I'll be on Mull, he told himself. Providing there are no more unpleasant surprises waiting for me on the way.

It was half past nine by the time Jake left the car-hire firm in Glasgow at the wheel of a small car. He'd been waiting outside their doors when they opened at eight thirty, but then a whole hour had been taken up with filling in forms.

No one attacked him as he left the forecourt. No one crashed into him. No one seemed to be watching him; but then that was difficult to be sure of in a city as busy as Glasgow.

The motorway through Glasgow was a nightmare for Jake, with intersections every half a mile or so, and traffic criss-crossing lanes. Once he was out of the city and heading along the road winding round Loch Lomond, he felt he could relax. He didn't spot any particular vehicle in his rear-view mirror as he drove. No one seemed to be following him. He was on his way.

As he drove he thought about Lauren, and how their lives had brought them to this. They'd met the year before, when Jake had been a trainee press officer at the Department of Science in London, and Lauren was a second-year science student at London University. It was love at first sight, and for six months Jake had been the happiest man in London, thinking their love was for ever. And then he'd ruined it.

A friend of Lauren's was getting married, and he and Lauren had gone to the wedding ceremony and the reception. It had seemed to Jake that Lauren spent an awful lot of time talking to some rugby-playing bloke she knew. Too much time. Smiling at him, laughing, touching his arm, even flicking her fingers through his hair as she pretended to examine his scalp for nits. Robert was his name. Robert the rugby player. And Jake had got fed up with it. And he did the unforgivable. He went off and found one of the bridesmaids, who'd already given him the eye earlier during the ceremony, and he'd got off with her in the bushes behind the drinks tent. Where Lauren had discovered them when she'd come looking for him.

He shuddered even now as he thought about it. He'd tried using the excuse that he was drunk, but it hadn't washed. It hadn't deserved to. Because of that one stupid act it was over. Lauren told him she never wanted to see him again. And then, afterwards, he'd found out that Robert wasn't a former boyfriend of Lauren's but her cousin. They'd been playmates since they'd been small children.

It had been the hidden library of Malichea that had brought them back together again, after three months, during which time Lauren had rejected all his attempts to get in touch with her.

The Order of Malichea. A blessing and a curse. A blessing because, if it hadn't been for the hidden books, Jake might never have seen Lauren again. But at the same time a curse, because their nightmare experiences after they'd got hold of one of the books — chased by government agents, under threat from mysterious organisations, likely international criminals and terrorists — had led to Lauren stabbing someone to death while defending herself against a deadly attack. And now she was in New Zealand, living under an assumed name, Samantha Adams, and they'd been told that she and Jake must never see one another again. If they attempted to, then Lauren would be charged with murder. The insinuation from Jake's former boss at the Department of Science was that Lauren would be found guilty, whatever her defence, and put away in jail for life. And Jake would be locked away somewhere secure.

The hidden library of Malichea was a forbidden topic. The British government had decided that its existence must never be allowed to be made public — the sciences the books contained were considered far too dangerous — and Jake and Lauren had posed a major threat to that secret. To make sure they didn't pose that threat ever again, they were kept on opposite sides of the globe, their phone calls, letters, emails and Skype talks monitored for any hint of discussion about the hidden books.

It had been five months since Jake had last seen Lauren face to face, held her in his arms just before she was put on the flight to New Zealand at Heathrow. Since then he'd seen her face on their Skype calls, heard her voice on the phone, but nothing took away the ache he

19

felt for her. They'd been reunited, only to be torn apart again. And now they were further apart than ever.

The drive to Oban took much longer than Jake had anticipated. The roads twisted and turned round lochs and rivers, in between mountains and high hills. The scenery was amazing. If he hadn't been in such a desperate hurry to get to Mull, meet this Miss Cooper and find out what had happened to Lauren, the reason for her sudden silence, he would have taken much longer over the journey.

He made it to Oban in time for the 4 p.m. ferry, and an hour later he was rolling off with the other vehicles into the tiny port of Craignure.

For the whole drive from Craignure to Craigmount Guest House on the shores of Loch Spelve, Jake was forced to keep a slow speed: the road was single-track, with passing places to allow oncoming vehicles to get past one another. The road twisted and turned as well, so it was impossible to get up any speed, without having to slow for yet another bend.

Finally he saw a cluster of buildings ahead of him, spread apart. Most were single-storey bungalows and old cottages, but there was one old two-storey house, larger than the rest, with outbuildings and gardens radiating out from it. A large cheerful wooden sign by the side of the road saying *Craigmount Guest House 200 metres* confirmed his destination.

There were four cars already in the car park, so there were other guests staying here. He wondered if one of them was this Miss Cooper's. He got out of his car, lifted out his bag, and entered the reception area of the guest house. A man with a big bushy grey beard was behind the desk, sorting through some papers. He looked up and smiled as Jake came in.

'Good afternoon!' he said.

'Good afternoon,' said Jake. 'I have a reservation. The name's Wells, Jake Wells.'

'Of course, we've been expecting you. You spoke to my wife, Jeannie, yesterday on the phone. I'm Alec MacClain, owner of Craigmount.'

He held out his hand in greeting, and Jake shook it. It was a good strong handshake, welcoming.

'You live in a beautiful part of the world,' said Jake admiringly.

'Aye, and we bless ourselves every morning and say the same thing to one another.' MacClain beamed. 'I'm sure, after your long journey, you'll want to get freshened up. Miss Cooper said to send you right up as soon as you arrived.'

'Thank you,' said Jake. 'Where is Miss Cooper?'

'She's in your room,' said MacClain. He reached for a key, attached to a wooden marker on a board and handed it to Jake. 'Room five. Turn right at the top of the stairs.'

21

'Thank you,' said Jake, and he followed the direction of MacClain's pointing finger. As he mounted the stairs, his mind was in a whirl. What was she doing waiting for him in his room? Why not in reception? It could only mean she had something private to tell him, something about Lauren she didn't want anyone else to overhear.

He moved faster up the carpeted stairs. Whatever news she had for him about Lauren, he needed to know. And he needed to know *now*.

He reached room five, put the key in the lock, opened the door, and stepped in. And stopped dead.

Lauren was there. Standing in front of him, turning towards him, her face lighting up with joy, her arms reaching out to him.

22

Chapter 4

Later, as Jake was making coffee, reality kicked in. 'How did you get here?' he asked, astonished.

'I flew.' Lauren grinned.

'Yes, but . . . you know what I mean. How did you get past passport control in New Zealand? How did you get through immigration control?'

She smiled and tugged at her hair, which was now short and blonde.

'Notice anything different?' she asked.

'You can't get in and out just by cutting and dying your hair!' exploded Jake. 'Not when you're on the Most Wanted list!'

'I did it with this,' said Lauren, and she reached into the drawer of the bedside table, took out a passport, and tossed it to Jake. Jake opened it, and saw a photo of a girl who *might* have resembled Lauren, but only just. Yes, this girl had short blonde hair. And there was something similar about the shape of her face. But to fool immigration, and MI5 . . .

'Helen Cooper,' explained Lauren. 'She lives in the same apartment block as me, and we became friends. I told her all about Malichea, the hidden science texts, and what had happened to us, and how you and I would never see each other again, and how desperate I was . . .'

'*We* were,' corrected Jake. As he carried the coffees towards the small table, he almost stumbled on the old and uneven wooden floor.

'Careful you don't spill them,' said Lauren.

Jake grinned.

'Nagging me already?' he asked.

'You need it,' she said. 'You get in trouble without me to look after you.'

'I get in trouble when we're together.' Jake smiled. 'So, how did you get to be Helen Cooper?'

'It was Helen who suggested it,' said Lauren. 'She commented one day about how similar we looked.'

Jake looked at the passport photo and shook his head.

'She's nowhere near as beautiful as you,' he said.

'You're only saying that because you're biased,' said Lauren. 'And anyway, passport photographs never show people at their best. She said if I was so desperate to get back to England and see you, why didn't I try using her passport. They'd be looking to stop Samantha Adams, or Lauren Graham, not Helen Cooper.'

'A woman with three identities,' commented Jake. 'Don't you sometimes forget who you really are?'

Lauren nodded.

'Sometimes,' she admitted. 'Sometimes, at work, when people call me Sam, just for the briefest of seconds I look around and wonder who they're talking to.' She gave Jake a stern look. 'That's why it's important we don't have any slip-ups while we're here. I'm Helen Cooper. Call me Helen all the time, even if we think we're alone. You never know who may be listening.'

'Even now?' asked Jake.

Lauren thought it over.

'It might be a good idea,' she said. 'To get used to it.'

Jake looked doubtful.

'I don't know if I'll ever get used to it,' he said. 'To me, you'll always be Lauren.'

'And I'll be Lauren again, once we get past this,' she assured him. 'Anyway, back to the passport. The more I thought about it, the stronger the appeal to try it became. I couldn't tell you, or even drop a hint, because, well . . .'

'They're listening.' Jake nodded.

'Yes,' said Lauren. 'So I decided to give it a try. Helen and I agreed that, if I was stopped and caught anywhere along the way, I'd say I'd stolen her passport from her, so she wouldn't get in trouble.'

'I phoned your work because I was worried I hadn't heard from you,' said Jake.

'I didn't dare tell *anyone*, apart from Helen,' said Lauren. 'For all we know they've got someone at my work, reporting back. Anyway, I booked the flights in Helen's name, and on the day I did my hair, set off, and just kept my fingers crossed.'

'You could have told me once you were back in England,' said Jake. 'We could have travelled up here together.'

Lauren shook her head.

'There were two reasons for that,' she said. 'One, I had this idea it might be easier to fly in from somewhere other than New Zealand. I hoped they'd be less vigilant about watching for me than if I went straight to London. So, I flew to Ireland first, and then from Ireland to Glasgow. The second was what the Russians are up to.'

'The Russians?' queried Jake.

'A party of them are here, on Mull! They're looking for one of the hidden books! And they've got a good idea where it is.'

Jake frowned, puzzled.

'Mull's a bit of a trek from Glastonbury, especially in medieval times,' he commented.

26

'Ah, that's because this book isn't from the secret library at Glastonbury!' said Lauren. 'There was another branch of the Order of Malichea set up on Iona!'

'That's the small island to the west of Mull.' Jake nodded.

'It was set up at the same time as the Order on Lindisfarne, in the eighth century.'

'I'm guessing this other branch of the Order of Malichea on Iona had a library as well?' asked Jake.

'Yes. The same as at Lindisfarne — scientific texts. In the case of the monastery on Iona, most of the writings came from Ireland, and the Celtic countries. But in addition there were texts from the Americas! Sciences from Native Americans, both north and south. Mayan. Aztec. Inca.'

Jake stared at her, stunned.

'But . . . how did they get them?' he asked. 'I can see travellers coming from the Continent, even the Mediterranean. But across the Atlantic?'

'Don't you know about the early sailors? The Brendan boat crossing the Atlantic?'

'No,' admitted Jake.

'I'll tell you about that later,' said Lauren. 'The main thing is, the science books were on Iona. And, just the same as the monks did at Lindisfarne, when they realised the Vikings were on their way to attack their monastery, they made sure their books were protected. But unlike at Lindisfarne, where they moved the library to another abbey for safe keeping, the monks on Iona hid their books at different places around the Highlands and islands. Travel from Iona wasn't as easy as it was from Lindisfarne and the north-east of England in those days.'

'It still isn't,' said Jake. 'Once you get past Glasgow, it still takes for ever!'

He sat there, letting all this sink in. The Order of Malichea was an ancient order, set up in the seventh century, devoted to building a library of scientific discoveries. In England the Order had run into trouble because the scientific texts they collected included topics such as invisibility, astronomy, time travel, as well as proposed cures for different diseases. Many of the theories in the texts were seen by the kings and the Church at the time as heretical, and so the library from the Order of Malichea based first at Lindisfarne, then at Glastonbury, had been hidden to protect them. To make sure that no one found the individual books, they had been hidden by the monks of the Order at sites said to be sacred, cursed or haunted, so they wouldn't be disturbed accidentally. That had been in 1497.

The abbey on Iona hadn't had the chance to build up a library to match the one at Glastonbury. The Vikings had attacked and destroyed Lindisfarne in 793. They swept into southern Scotland a year later, continuing their path of destruction. So the scientific texts from the abbey at Iona must have been buried 700 years before those from Glastonbury.

'We are talking about *really* old books,' said Jake.

'Not even books, at that time,' said Lauren. 'Not as we know them. Scrolls. Parchment.' She gave Jake a small smile of triumph. 'And what's more, I know which particular text the Russians are looking for.'

Jake stared at her.

'How?' he asked.

'Chatter on the web,' said Lauren.

'How could you follow all this on the web without MI5 closing down your computer?' asked Jake.

'Cybercafés, you idiot,' said Lauren. 'And using Helen's computer. Anyway, the book they're after is *De Materia Medica Continuum* by Dioscorides. It was written in AD 53, and is about spontaneous human combustion.' She shrugged. 'Why it went to Iona and not to Lindisfarne, no one seems to know. Maybe the person who brought it had a personal connection with someone at the monastery on Iona. But the fact is that *this* is the book they're looking for. They're using the cover of pretending to dig for Neolithic remains at the site.' She gave a snort. 'Very clever.'

'But how do the Russians know what this particular book is called, and where it is?' asked Jake, puzzled.

'That's the really important thing!' said Lauren

excitedly. 'Don't you see, Jake? It means they've got hold of The Index!'

'The Index?'

'The journal that lists every book that was in the library at the monastery on Iona, and where it was buried!'

Chapter 5

Jake sat, stunned. So much information, and raising so many questions.

'Actually, the Russians must have only got hold of part of The Index, otherwise they'd be all over the Highlands and islands, digging everywhere.'

'But why would the Russians be interested in . . . what was it again?'

'Spontaneous human combustion. Where a human being just bursts into flames from the inside, and gets burnt to ashes.'

Jake shuddered.

'Weird,' he muttered.

'It's not weird,' said Lauren. 'It's some sort of chemical reaction inside the body, triggered by something. There are lots of instances of it recorded, but no one knows why it happens. It may be that Dioscorides had the answer.'

'OK, but back to my original question: why would the Russians be interested in it?'

'The Russians have always been interested in what you used to call "weird science",' said Lauren. 'In the Soviet era they had whole government science departments carrying out experiments on things like telepathy, telekinesis, levitation.'

'Why?'

'One, to get an understanding of how and why things work. And, two, to see if any of them could be used as weapons. Just think, if you had a telepath inside the White House, you wouldn't need electronic surveillance — very expensive and easy to discover.'

'And spontaneous human combustion? People bursting into flames?'

'Can you think of a better weapon?' asked Lauren.

'No,' admitted Jake. 'So, what are we going to do here?'

'We're going to wait until the Russians find the book, and then get it back off them. And we're going to see if we can get whatever part of The Index they have off them as well. There are bound to be other books listed in it. They're going to be our bargaining chips.'

'To get you back here?'

Lauren nodded. 'Back properly, under my own name, so we can be together openly. And prove that the secret library of Malichea exists.'

'That the library on *Iona* existed,' stressed Jake.

'It's a start,' said Lauren. 'First we prove that there was an Order of Malichea on Iona who buried their library; then that gets the whole business of the Order and their secret library out into the open.'

Jake nodded.

'Sounds like a good plan,' he said. 'How are we going to get the book off the Russians once they find it?'

'That's what we've got to work out,' she said. 'Tomorrow I'll take you along to the site where they're digging, and then we'll have a look at the cottage where the Russians are staying, and we can work out how we're going to do it.'

'We're going to have opposition,' said Jake. 'Let's face it, if you know about this, so will everyone else who's interested. MI5. The CIA. Pierce Randall. The Watchers.'

'Yes,' agreed Lauren. 'I've been trying to work out who might be who. There's an American staying here. Ian Muir. He says he's come here to explore his Scottish roots, but it wouldn't surprise me to find out he's CIA. Then there's a couple of Brits, Mr and Mrs Gordon, John and Pam. Very nice. They claim they're here bird-watching. They say they're here especially to see golden eagles.'

'MI5?'

'Possibly. Or they could be working for Pierce Randall. We know how far that bunch of crooked lawyers will go

33

to get their hands on the books. Their clients are some of the richest people on the planet, so Pierce Randall can make a lot of money finding the books for them.'

'What about the Watchers?'

The Watchers, the mysterious organisation set up hundreds of years before to keep guard over the hidden books and protect them from being found.

'I'm fairly sure the MacClains who run this place are Watchers,' said Lauren. 'The family have been here for generations, stretching right back to the time the books were hidden. They must be involved in some way.'

'OK.' Jake nodded. 'So those are the ones we know about.'

'*Suspect*,' corrected Lauren. 'I could be wrong about any or all of them. And, of course, there are loads of other people on the island. Mull is a haven for visitors, birdwatchers, tourists, people who want to get away from things. And Iona is a must for pilgrims as well as tourists. Any of them could be using that as a cover while they keep watch on the Russian dig.'

'And try and get their hands on the book,' mused Jake.

Lauren nodded.

'Well, I guess that's the answer to why things happened to me when I tried to come up here,' said Jake.

'What do you mean?' asked Lauren.

'I got warned off. And then attacked, at Euston, just as I was about to get on my train.' He shuddered at the all-too-recent memory. 'They tried to stab me, but luckily their knife got my bag instead.'

Lauren stared at him, horrified.

'Who were they?' she asked.

Jake shrugged.

'I don't know,' he said. 'But obviously someone didn't want me joining in the fun.'

'How did they know?'

'That's easy,' said Jake. 'They eavesdrop. They know everything.' He grinned. 'Except the fact that Lauren Graham is back and pretending to be Helen Cooper.'

'Yes, and, like I said, we need to keep it that way,' said Lauren.

Then a worrying thought struck Jake.

'With all these different interested parties here, you don't think one of them might recognise you?'

'Blonde hair? Helen Cooper? I hope not,' said Lauren. 'I'm hoping their attention will be on the Russians.'

'OK,' said Jake. 'But if we manage to get hold of this book, then all attention is going to switch to us. We need an escape plan to get us off this island at speed.'

'I know,' said Lauren.

'Have you got one?' asked Jake.

'No,' admitted Lauren. 'But I'm working on it.'

Chapter 6

At breakfast the next morning, Jake and Lauren, and the two birdwatchers, Pam and John Gordon, were the only ones in the dining room. The American, Ian Muir, had apparently already had his breakfast and left.

'He says he likes to be out there before anyone else,' Lauren said. 'The early bird catches the worm, that sort of thing. He says all the best things in nature happen around dawn.'

'Or, he gets a chance to watch the Russians before anyone else is in action,' murmured Jake.

'That's my guess,' said Lauren.

'If he is CIA, I can't imagine him working alone,' said Jake.

'I thought of that. He must have a contact somewhere else nearby,' agreed Lauren. 'We'll be passing the cottages I told you about on the way to the dig site. His contact could be there.'

'So why isn't he with them?' asked Jake.

Lauren shrugged.

'Maybe they've got people in different places all over the island, watching what's going on. Staying close to the opposition,' she suggested.

'Keeping an eye on another pair of prime suspects?' whispered Jake, and he turned and smiled at Pam and John Gordon, who were sitting at a table at the far side of the dining room. The couple smiled back.

'Lovely day for going out walking!' called Pam Gordon.

'It certainly is!' Lauren said.

Before they could embark on a long conversation, Jeannie MacClain appeared by their table, notepad at the ready.

'Are you ready to order?' she asked.

They gave her their orders: a full Scots for Jake, and cereal followed by kippers for Lauren.

'Excellent!' Their hostess beamed. 'My daughter Rona's helping me in the kitchen today. A full breakfast will give her something to keep her busy.'

'Mr and Mrs MacClain have run this guest house for twenty years,' said Lauren.

'It's a beautiful place,' said Jake. 'But it must be lonely for you out of season.'

'No, there's always something to do,' said Jeannie. 'Repairs, renovation, decorating. Making sure we've got enough fuel for the winter months. And there are always people who want to come to Mull in the winter months, especially around Christmas and Hogmanay time. Believe me, island life is far from lonely. I have a sister who lives in Edinburgh, and when I visit her it's often struck me that city life is far lonelier for many people, even with all those thousands crammed in one small space.'

'She's got a point,' said Jake, as Jeannie MacClain went to the Gordons' table to take their breakfast order. He lowered his voice and asked: 'So, if the MacClains are Watchers, how many of them are there? I've met Mrs MacClain's husband, Alec, and their daughter Rona's in the kitchen.'

'She's fifteen,' said Lauren. 'She's working here during the school holidays. Then there's their son, Robbie. He's sixteen. He spends most of his time with his uncle, Alec MacClain's younger brother, Dougie. Dougie's a fisherman, plus general handyman, does odd jobs around the island.'

'Ideal cover for a Watcher,' murmured Jake.

'Exactly what I thought,' said Lauren.

After a breakfast that was so huge, Jake was sure he wouldn't need to eat anything again for a couple of days, they put on their boots and anoraks, packed a small rucksack with provisions provided by Jeannie

38

MacClain, and notebooks, maps and a guide book, and with binoculars hanging around their necks, set off. They were heading for the dig where the Russians were claiming to be unearthing an ancient Neolithic site.

As Jake and Lauren stepped out of the guest house, once again he was struck by the vastness of the sky above them; it wasn't something he had ever thought about living in London and the south-east. But here, there was so much space!

They walked along the road, past a small group of holiday cottages, and then turned off on to a path that rambled across a vast expanse of heathland. Wild flowers were everywhere, and huge bushes exploding in a riot of colours.

'Wow!' said Jake. 'What are they?'

'Rhododendrons. It's a parasite,' said Lauren dismissively. 'It poisons the ground and kills off other plants.'

'So why do they allow so many of them to grow?' asked Jake. 'They're everywhere!'

'Because once they've been planted, it's almost impossible to get rid of them,' said Lauren. 'You have to dig up the roots, and if you leave a piece of the root in the ground it'll spread very fast. But the Victorian plant hunters didn't realise that when they brought them back to Britain. Like you, they just saw a plant that looked beautiful. But beauty often hides a secret killer.'

'And on that grim note . . .' muttered Jake.

They continued on the path for almost two miles, and suddenly they were out of the bushes and saw, about half a mile ahead of them, an almost industrial monstrosity: a wire fence over three metres tall, topped with razor wire, surrounding a large area.

'What on earth is that?' burst out Jake.

'That is the Russians' dig site,' said Lauren.

'What? In a beautiful place like this! How did they get permission for it?'

'How do rich Russians get permission for anything?' asked Lauren. 'Planning permission for a fence like that in a conservation area like this. Or a controlling monopoly interest in some nationalised industry.'

'You're suggesting money talks?'

Lauren nodded.

'Exactly. It's an international language.'

As they drew nearer to the site, Jake could see a small party of about half a dozen people at work, two digging and the rest crouching down and sifting through the earth that had been turned over.

'It's a massive site,' murmured Jake.

'Which means they don't know the exact spot where the book was buried, just the general area where it was hidden,' said Lauren.

By now they had reached the fence. They walked along it until they came to a gap, an open gateway. A piece of rope had been hung across the gateway to stop people from wandering in. Jake and Lauren stopped by the rope and looked into the site. Some sections of the area had already been dug up; there were mounds of earth dotted all over the site. But it was being searched methodically, and about half of the site had been uncovered: the topsoil turned over and the rocks beneath exposed.

'It doesn't look much like a Neolithic site,' murmured Jake.

'Who can tell what a Neolithic site looks like?' responded Lauren. 'They didn't plan their buildings the same way later civilisations did.'

Just then there was an angry shout.

'Go away!'

They turned and saw a man approaching them from within the fenced-off area, a grim scowl on his face.

'Pardon?' asked Jake.

The man arrived by them, on the other side of the rope. He was short and squat, dressed in what looked like a navy-blue boiler suit. He pointed a stubby finger at them and repeated: 'Go away! Private property.'

'I don't think so,' said Jake. 'It may be on that side of the rope, but not where we're standing.'

'Dmitri!' came another voice.

And then another man was hurrying towards them, this one older, taller, thinner, and with an apologetic expression on his face. The short squat man, Dmitri, turned and looked at the new arrival, the scowl on his face even deeper. The taller man stopped by the rope and said something to Dmitri in rapid Russian. Even though Jake and Lauren couldn't understand the words, they recognised the firm tone. The tall man finished talking, and Dmitri nodded, turned on his heel, and went back into the centre of the dig site, still scowling. The tall man gave Jake and Lauren a friendly smile.

'I must apologise for Dmitri,' he said. 'His English is limited, and as a result he can only say a few words, which means he can come across as rude and brusque. He's not like that at all, really.'

I bet, thought Jake sceptically, watching the short squat figure stomp away. The man in the blue boiler suit looked like a wrestler, the sort who threw his opponents out of the ring.

'I hear you're digging for Neolithic remains,' said Jake.

'Yes.' The tall man nodded. He held out his hand to them with a smile. 'Professor Fyodor Lemski,' he introduced himself.

Jake shook the man's hand; then it was Lauren's turn.

'I have seen you here before,' said Lemski to Lauren. 'You were here yesterday, and the day before, I believe, watching from a distance.'

'Yes,' said Lauren. 'I was curious about what you were doing, but was too shy to ask.'

Jake grinned.

'I don't have those same kind of inhibitions.' He beamed at the professor.

'You are interested in archaeology?' asked Lemski.

'Very much so.' Jake nodded. 'Both of us.' He gestured into the site where the people were at work. 'Perhaps we could come and see what you're doing up close?'

Jake thought he saw a momentary flicker of alarm in the professor's face, then the smile was back in place, as apologetic as before.

'Unfortunately, much as I would love to, we are hampered by insurance.'

'Insurance?' queried Lauren.

Lemski nodded.

'As part of our getting permission to dig, we had to take out insurance to cover against accidents or anything going wrong. And the terms of our insurance are very strict, only our own people are allowed on the site.' He sighed unhappily as he gestured at the towering wire fence. 'Which is why we were forced to erect this terrible fence. It appears that despite warning signs being put up, some people have been known to creep into archaeological sites under cover of darkness and have fallen down where digging has taken place, and have unfortunately been seriously injured. Some have even been killed.'

'No!' exclaimed Jake.

Lemski nodded, his expression sad.

'And if that were to happen here, we would be held responsible.' He shrugged. 'It is the way of the world, now. Everyone sues. So, I am sorry I cannot invite you in. But, rest assured, we will be publishing a report of our findings for all to see.'

'Excellent,' said Lauren. 'We look forward to seeing it.' She turned to Jake. 'We'd better get on.' To Lemski, she explained, 'We're going down to the cove to explore the caves, and we don't want to get cut off by the tide.'

'Of course.' Lemski nodded. 'It was a pleasure to meet you both.'

As Jake and Lauren walked away, Lauren whispered, 'So we're warned off, with a smile from the professor, and a scowl from Mr Grumpy in the blue boiler suit.'

'I think Mr Grumpy is armed,' whispered back Jake. 'I'm sure I saw the outline of a shoulder holster.'

'Yes, I spotted that too. So, definite keep-out warnings, and armed security. Notice how he subtly mentioned people being killed at archaeological sites?'

'I'd hardly call that subtle,' said Jake. 'Why would he feel it necessary to warn us off like that, do you think? We're supposed to be just two ordinary holiday-makers. Do we look suspicious?'

44

'To people like the professor, who are searching for the book, everyone is suspicious,' said Lauren.

Suddenly she stopped, her attention caught by something.

'What have you seen?' asked Jake.

'Someone creeping around on the far side of the site, behind those rocks.'

'One of the Russians?' asked Jake.

Lauren shook her head.

'It looked like Mr Muir. The American I told you about.'

'How can you tell from this distance?' asked Jake.

'He's got a distinctive way of moving. A limp.'

Jake wasn't convinced.

'From this distance, how can you tell that someone moving across those rocks moves with a limp or not?' he asked.

'It's hard to say,' said Lauren. 'It's just a feeling. You'll see what I mean when you meet him this evening. He's usually in the bar.'

'The CIA keeping watch?' asked Jake.

'I would imagine that everyone's keeping watch,' said Lauren.

Chapter 7

As they left the dig site behind them, Jake asked, 'What was all that about going down to the cove?'

'It seemed like a good idea to move on before he started asking too many questions about us,' replied Lauren. 'Also, the cove is a great place. Beautiful. And the tide does come in quite rapidly.'

Jake followed Lauren along a rough track, then they turned off on to a path that suddenly started to descend, twisting and turning through the cliffs as it went down. Thick bushes and bramble bordered the path, growing out of the rocks, screening any view. The ground underfoot was loose stones, and Jake had to use his hands to steady himself against the rock face a few times. Finally they made it down to level ground, and as Jake stepped off the path, he stopped, stunned by the view: the sea loch directly in front of him, and the hills and mountains covered in purple and green in the distance on the other side of the loch. The rocks gave way to white sands, going down to the shore. Birds wheeled overhead.

'I'm told that you can see otters in the water if you come down here early enough,' said Lauren. 'And deer, who come down to the loch side, in the evening, just before nightfall.'

'Wow!' said Jake.

This place was a whole world away from the crowded streets of London, where he'd spent all his life. It had a peace and tranquillity he'd never experienced before. And yet, just a few hundred metres away up the path from the shore, an excavation was at work, looking for a book that could hold the key to making one of the most potentially dangerous weapons ever known. What was it Lauren had said? *Beauty often hides a secret killer.*

'We can get back to the guest house along the shore,' Lauren said. 'There's another path a couple of miles along here that goes back up to the cliff top.'

'Another couple of miles?' echoed Jake, horrified. 'We'll have walked about six miles today! And we'll be finishing with a climb upwards!'

Lauren smiled.

'It'll make you fit,' she teased him.

'It'll make me exhausted,' countered Jake.

But, as they walked and he took in the scenery all

around them, Jake had to admit it was worth it. I wish we could be here without us needing to find the book, he thought. Without the Russians and MI5 and the CIA, and everyone else, and all this intrigue. I wish it could be just me and Lauren, walking along the shore like this, free and without any worries. And he reached out and took Lauren's hand in his, and squeezed it gently; and she squeezed back.

'There's Robbie!' she exclaimed. 'And his Uncle Dougie!'

Jake saw two small upturned boats on the shore ahead of them, with two figures working on one of them. As they neared them, they saw that they were painting the upturned hull of the boat.

'Good morning!' called Lauren brightly.

The two stopped their painting and turned. The older of the two, Dougie MacClain, gave a friendly smile.

'Good morning, Miss Cooper!' He beamed.

'This is my friend, Jake Wells,' said Lauren.

'Hi!' said Jake, and he held out his hand.

Dougie looked down at his own hand, then shook Jake's hand. His handshake was firm and friendly, like his brother Alec's had been.

'Just checking I didn't have paint on it,' he explained.

'I could always wash it off,' said Jake.

'Not this stuff,' chuckled Dougie. 'Special paint for

boats. Hard stuff. Has to be to withstand the salt in the sea. Isn't that right, Robbie?'

Robbie nodded. Unlike his uncle, he didn't smile.

He doesn't trust us, thought Jake.

'We've just met the Russians at their dig site,' said Lauren.

'Aye?' said Dougie cautiously.

'Dreadful!' exploded Jake. 'That fence shouldn't be allowed in a beautiful place like this!'

'The whole thing shouldn't be allowed,' growled Robbie. 'They're digging up sacred ground! People died there where they're digging. They should be left in peace!'

'Robbie feels very strongly about it.' Dougie smiled.

'I don't blame him,' said Jake. 'I'd feel the same if I was him.'

Get on their side, thought Jake. If the MacClains were Watchers, as Lauren suspected, then they'd be keeping a close watch on the site, and everyone going near it. He and Lauren might well need their help.

'What's the fishing like?' Jake asked Dougie, indicating the boats.

Dougie shook his head sadly.

'Non-existent,' he said. 'It's nearly all salmon farming these days. Everything seems to be on an industrial scale.'

49

'No room for the small fisherman,' sighed Jake sympathetically.

'We get by,' said Dougie. He smiled at Robbie. 'Robbie wants to join me when he leaves school. I've told him there's no future here. He ought to go to university and get a degree in something. Make his future elsewhere, where the money is.'

'My future's here,' said Robbie firmly. 'This is my home. If you can make a living here, so can I.'

'There's always tourism,' said Lauren.

'And archaeologists.' Jake grinned.

Robbie scowled, not amused.

'Come on, Robbie,' said Dougie. 'We'd better get on with this before the paint starts to dry. Have a good day, Miss Cooper. Nice to meet you, Mr Wells.'

Dougie and Robbie turned back to their painting, and Jake and Lauren continued their walk along the shore.

'Well, what do you think?' whispered Lauren. 'D'you think Dougie's a Watcher?'

'With the small number of residents on this island, especially those with a long ancestry here, that makes sense to me,' agreed Jake.

Chapter 8

That evening, Jake and Lauren found themselves comfortable seats in the small bar area, and were just toasting one another with drinks, when a short but stocky man came over to them, holding a drink in his hand. Jake saw that he walked with a slight limp. This must be Muir, thought Jake. The mysterious American.

It was confirmed as the man gave them a smile of greeting, and said to Jake in an American accent: 'Hi, I'm Ian Muir. You must be Jake. Miss Cooper said you were coming. Do you mind if I join you?'

'Not at all,' said Jake, gesturing at the empty chair.

'Can I get you folks a drink?' asked Muir.

Jake and Lauren shook their heads.

'We're fine, thanks, Mr Muir,' said Lauren.

'Ian, please,' said Muir.

He put his own glass down on the table, and made himself comfortable in the chair.

'Some island, huh?' he asked.

'It certainly is,' agreed Jake.

Muir took a sip of his drink, then said: 'I saw you talking to our Russian friends at their dig today. You interested in archaeology as well, Jake?'

'I certainly am,' said Jake.

'Mind, if you ask me, the Russians are lucky to be able to just turn up and dig like that. No red tape, no form-filling, just get right on with it.'

'I'm sure it's not that simple,' said Lauren. 'I expect they had to make submissions before they could dig, just like anyone else.'

'I hear what you say.' Muir nodded. 'But I bet you they got their permissions faster and easier than most. And with less restrictions. Look at that fence they've put up, for one thing! What an eyesore! On a beautiful place like this!'

Jake smiled at Lauren. Muir was echoing her own sentiments about the dig.

'But then the system here in Scotland's still pretty feudal,' continued Muir. 'Throw the local laird enough money, and you can do pretty much anything. Providing you grease a few palms of the local councillors and members of the Scottish Parliament.'

'I get the impression you don't have much time for the people in power locally,' said Jake.

'No, Jake, I don't,' said Muir. 'I come back here, and

52

it seems not a lot's changed since the Clearances forcibly kicked out my great-great-great-grandfather and sent him off to Canada back in the 1800s.' He obviously saw Jake's puzzled expression, because he asked: 'You don't know about the Clearances? The Highlanders were evicted from their homes and sent to Canada and Australia just so the landowners could graze sheep on the land.'

'No,' admitted Jake.

'You don't know about the history of your own country?' asked Muir accusingly.

'I'm English,' said Jake. 'This is Scotland.'

'But isn't it all the same country?' asked Muir. 'The United Kingdom?'

'That depends who you talk to,' said Jake. 'As far as many of the Scots and Welsh are concerned, no. Their countries are separate. Hence the independence movements.' He frowned. 'But I'm surprised we haven't heard about these Clearances. Every day there seems to be some new revelation of the bad things the Imperial English did in the past to other nations. The famine in Ireland. Suppression of the Welsh. Massacres in India.'

Muir chuckled.

'This wasn't the English. It was the Scots doing it to themselves. Scottish landowners, the Scottish aristocracy, getting rid of Scottish peasants.'

53

'Ah,' nodded Jake in understanding, 'that explains it.'

'Calgary in Alberta in Canada is actually named after Calgary Bay here on Mull, because it was from that same bay that many of the ships went across the Atlantic, taking the Highlanders to their new life,' said Muir. His expression clouded as he added, 'Those who didn't get on the ships voluntarily were hunted down by dogs, and then bound hand and foot and thrown on board.'

'But you're American,' said Lauren. 'I thought you said your great-great-great-grandfather went to Canada.'

'He did,' agreed Muir. 'But two of his sons crossed the border and settled in Chicago, thinking life might offer greater opportunities for them there. And that's where my particular branch of the family comes from. The Windy City.' He sipped his drink. 'Most people have no idea the impact that Scotland has had on North America, both sides of the border. Most Canadians are either from Scots or French descent, mainly Scots. And the States wouldn't be anywhere without the Scots!' He leant forward. 'Remember the moon landing in 1969?'

'Not personally,' said Jake. 'Way before I was born. But I know about it, obviously.'

Muir didn't seem to have heard him, he continued with what was becoming almost a lecture: 'At the ceremony to celebrate the moon landing, the three men on the podium were the astronaut Neil Armstrong,

President Richard Nixon, and the Reverend Billy Graham. All of Scottish descent.'

'The Clearances?' asked Jake.

Muir shook his head.

'No, the Reivers.'

'The Border Reivers.' Lauren nodded.

'I'm impressed.' Muir smiled at her. 'One of you knows their Scottish history.'

Lauren was on the point of retorting: 'I ought to know about the Reivers, I'm a Graham,' but she stopped herself in time. My name's Cooper, she reminded herself. Helen Cooper.

'The Border Reivers were clans who operated both sides of the Scottish and English border from the twelfth century to the seventeenth,' continued Muir. 'They were murderers and gangsters. They killed for profit and for power.'

'Just like modern organised crime,' said Lauren.

'Absolutely,' agreed Muir. 'Chicago, New York, London, Mexico. The story's the same.'

'But you say they did it for *five hundred* years,' said Jake.

'Because there was no law in that part of Britain,' said Muir.

'They called the border area the Debatable Lands,' added Lauren.

'Like I say, you know your history,' he said.

'So what happened to them?' asked Jake. 'They suddenly stopped?'

Muir gestured at Lauren. 'I'll let you tell him.'

'King James I of England offered the clans a deal: they could either join him and become his servants, swearing fealty and giving all their lands and goods to him, or they could be transported to the New World — America. Or they could be executed.'

Muir grinned.

'In the words of *The Godfather*, it was an offer they couldn't refuse. About half accepted the king's terms, and just under half accepted the offer of a new life in the American colonies.'

'What happened to the rest?'

'They were executed,' said Lauren. 'As an example to any others who might be considering rebelling.'

'An English king killing and exiling Scots,' murmured Jake. 'I'm surprised the Scots who want independence haven't made more of that.'

'He was King James VI of Scotland before he became King of England,' said Lauren. 'He was the son of Mary, Queen of Scots.'

'I see,' said Jake.

Muir grinned and raised his glass to them in a toast.

'See?' he said. 'Trust me, the Scots should spend more time blaming their own Scottish aristocracy for their troubles!'

Chapter 9

As they got back to their room, Jake's mind was still whirling with all the historical facts Muir had loaded them with during their session.

'Wow!' said Jake. 'That was some history lesson!'

'He's an expat,' explained Lauren. 'Expats and second-generation immigrants are always more patriotic about their mother country than the people who still live there.'

'Still think he's CIA?' asked Jake.

Lauren shrugged.

'If he is, his cover's good.'

'So, what next?'

Lauren smiled and came to Jake, and put her arms around him.

'After the history lesson, I was thinking of trying some biology,' she whispered.

'I always preferred biology,' he murmured.

*　*　*

Next morning, the sky was overcast, but Jake couldn't have cared less if it had been blowing a gale outside. He was here, with Lauren, and they were closer than they'd ever been.

After breakfast they set out for the site of the dig again, dressed for anything the weather might throw at them, and both with binoculars hanging around their necks.

'You think that professor might get suspicious if he sees us again?' asked Jake. 'I mean, we're supposed to be tourists.'

'Tourists interested in archaeology,' pointed out Lauren. 'Anyway, I thought we'd just give it a glance today, and go and check out the cottage where the Russians are staying.'

'Sounds like a plan,' said Jake.

Actually, he was happy to agree with anything that Lauren suggested. All right, they were here on a mission: to find the book. Or, to stop the Russians finding it. But the main thing for Jake was that they were together. Not stuttering images on a Skype window, or disembodied voices echoing down a tele-phone line, but holding hands, touching, looking at each other in the face and smiling and being close to one another.

They walked along the track that took them past the Russians' site, slowing down as they passed to see what was going on, whether there was any sense of excitement about the people working; but it was all as it had been the previous day: people digging, others in holes, using small trowels and brushes to scrape away earth, and the tall figure of Professor Lemski moving around, overseeing operations.

They followed the path for about another half a mile and reached a cliff top overlooking the loch. Here, the path separated, going in both directions along the edge. The path to the right would take them past a cottage and a few outbuildings.

'That's where the Russians are staying,' murmured Lauren.

'Then I think a stroll along the cliff path in that direction is what we need,' said Jake.

They set off. A low wire fence ran along the edge of the path, keeping people away from the cliff. The cottage where the Russian party was staying seemed quiet, but as they neared it Jake could make out people in the courtyard at the back of the cottage, and in some of the outbuildings. They looked up as Jake and Lauren walked by, and although he and she both smiled and waved at them, they gave no greeting back; just watched the pair suspiciously.

A movement on the marsh about a quarter of a mile inland suddenly caught Jake's eye.

'See that?' he said, stopping and looking.

'Keep moving,' urged Lauren. 'We don't want them to get suspicious.'

'They're already suspicious,' said Jake. 'Just look at the expressions on their faces. It's like they're expecting us to break in.'

'That's understandable,' said Lauren. 'After all, that's what we plan to do if they find it.'

'True,' admitted Jake.

They walked on, past the cottage and the outbuildings, until they rounded a bend and were out of sight.

'OK, we can stop now,' said Lauren. 'What did you see?'

'It looked like our friend Mr Ian Muir,' said Jake. 'I'm sure it was him heading across the marsh, away from the Russians' cottage.'

'And yesterday he was sneaking away from the dig,' added Lauren.

Jake stepped towards the fence and the cliff edge. He looked down towards the shore, looking out for the otters that Lauren had talked about, hoping to see them in the water. Instead, he saw something else that made him jerk back, alarmed.

'What's up?' asked Lauren.

'There's someone down there,' said Jake. 'And they look like they're hurt.'

Lauren went to the edge and peered down. A man was lying face down on the rocks below, arms spread out. He was wearing an old overcoat and rubber boots, and he wasn't moving.

'Which is the quickest way down from here?' asked Jake.

'This way,' said Lauren. She was already heading towards a gap in some bushes. Jake hurried after her, and they half climbed, half stumbled down a steep and rocky path that twisted and turned down the cliff. They reached the shore. On this side of the headland the beach was rocky rather than sand and shingle, and they hurried over the rocks towards the prone man, slipping as they went. As they got near him they saw the blood on the back of his skull. Jake felt a lurch of recognition as they got closer; the coat looked like the one Dougie MacClain had been wearing when they'd met him with Robbie the previous day.

They reached the man. His head was turned to one side. His eyes and mouth were open. It was Dougie MacClain all right, with blood matting his hair, and the flash of bone where his smashed skull was visible through the mess. Even before they tested for a pulse, they knew it was no good. He was dead.

Chapter 10

It's odd, thought Jake. Everything here on the island either happens at once, or it takes for ever. Lauren got a signal on her mobile and phoned the MacClains at the guest house and told them there had been a serious accident involving Dougie MacClain. She stressed that it was very serious, and advised against allowing either Robbie or Rona to come.

Despite her appeal, within minutes, Alec MacClain and Robbie had arrived in a battered old Land Rover. They hurried to the body of Dougie, and the despair was evident on their faces as they looked at him. Robbie, especially, was deathly white. Desperately, Alec searched for any sign of life, feeling for pulses on Dougie's neck and wrists, leaning close to check for any hint of breath; but it was all too obvious that life had gone.

Shortly afterwards, a search and rescue helicopter was seen approaching, and it settled down on the shore. Paramedics jumped out and rushed to Dougie, but the sense of urgent action faded as they realised he was dead. They took Dougie's body to the helicopter, muttered a few words to Alec, and then flew off.

The arrival of the police took a little longer. Alec told Lauren and Jake that a uniformed constable was on his way from the local station at Craignure. More police would be coming over from Oban by boat, but they would be delayed until the tide was high enough for them to be able to land.

Jake and Lauren climbed into the cab of the Land Rover, next to Alec, while Robbie climbed into the open back, and they headed back to the guest house.

As the Land Rover drew to a halt at the back of the guest house, Jeannie and Rona came hurrying out. Both had obviously been crying. Jeannie and Rona threw themselves into Alec's arms, and he hugged them to him. Robbie stayed in the back of the vehicle, his face white and shocked.

'We need to give them some space,' whispered Lauren.

Jake nodded, and they went up to their room.

'What do you think?' asked Jake once they were inside their own room. 'An accident, or was he killed?'

'Who would want to kill him?' asked Lauren.

'Where the books are involved, people are always dying,' said Jake. 'You and I both thought he may have

63

been a Watcher. The Watchers' job is to protect the books, stop them being discovered. Maybe he tried to stop this book being found, and was killed.'

'The Russians?'

Jake shrugged.

'Right now, I can't think of anyone else,' he said. 'They're the ones looking for the book.'

'What about Muir?' asked Lauren. 'We saw him acting suspiciously in that area.'

'Maybe,' agreed Jake. 'But what reason would he have for killing Dougie?'

'The book,' said Lauren. 'It's always about the books.'

A sergeant and a constable arrived by boat from the mainland an hour and a half after Dougie's body had been flown away. They joined the local constable from Craignure in the lounge of the guest house, which had been set up as the base for their investigation. The first people they wanted to talk to were Jake and Lauren.

'We'll see you one at a time, if you don't mind,' the sergeant told them. He nodded at Jake. 'We'll start with you first, sir.'

They want to question us separately and see if our stories match up, Jake thought.

Jake told the sergeant and the constable what he'd seen. Not that there was much to say, just that they'd been walking along the cliff and they'd spotted the body of Dougie MacClain lying at the bottom of it. There then followed questions about Jake himself. Why had he come to Mull? Jake and Lauren had already rehearsed their answers should these kind of questions come up: they were old friends meeting up on Mull for a holiday, once 'Helen Cooper' had decided to come to England from her home in New Zealand.

'What were you doing when you found Mr MacClain's body?'

'Just walking. Exploring the island.'

'Did you see anyone else in the area?'

'Not on the shore,' said Jake. 'The Russians were in their enclosure, doing their dig, at the top of the cliff.'

'Anyone else?'

'The American who's staying here,' said Jake. 'Mr Muir. We saw him.'

'On the shore?'

'No,' said Jake. 'I just said, we didn't see anyone else on the shore.'

'So where did you see Mr Muir?'

'Near the cottage where the Russians are staying.'

The sergeant looked at him quizzically.

'How come you know the Russians are staying there, sir?' he said. 'Do you have an interest in these Russians?'

Jake shook his head.

'It's a small island,' he said. 'Everyone seems to know who everyone else is. I thought it was easier than saying "In the cottage with the green door near the cliff edge". That could mean a lot of different cottages.'

The sergeant studied Jake thoughtfully.

'How do you know that cottage has got a green door, sir?' he asked. 'Have you been keeping a special eye on it?'

'I don't,' said Jake. 'I just said "green" to give you an example of what I meant. For all I know the door's red or yellow.' He frowned. 'Out of curiosity, what colour is the door?'

'Green, sir,' said the sergeant.

Jake smiled.

'Lucky guess,' he said.

The sergeant didn't smile back. Inwardly, Jake kicked himself. I've made him suspicious about what we're doing here, he thought. Let's hope they don't start digging too deeply into 'Helen Cooper'.

The interview carried on, mostly going over the same ground. He's asking me the same questions in a different way, seeing if I trip myself up, thought Jake. Luckily, Jake could repeat the fact about their discovery of Dougie McLain's body over and over again without a problem. He just told the sergeant what they'd seen, and what they'd done. Finally, after what seemed like an eternity, the sergeant said: 'Thank you sir. That'll be all for the moment.'

'Fine,' said Jake. 'I'll go and get . . .' He was about to say 'Lauren', when he stopped himself just in time, and said, 'Miss Cooper for you.'

'No need,' said the sergeant. 'The constable will tell her we're ready for her.'

In other words, they don't want us talking together before they get a chance to question her as well, thought Jake. They're still set on checking if our stories match up.

Jake left the lounge and strolled towards the back door of the guest house. In the small back garden there was a seat he could relax in without bumping into people like Muir, or Mr and Mrs Gordon. As he neared the open back door, he could hear angry voices just outside. Rona and Robbie.

'We know who did it!' he heard Rona say, blazing fury in her voice.

'We have to let the police do their job,' Robbie cautioned her.

Suddenly Jake felt an overpowering urge to talk to them, sweep away the pretence and tell them he knew what this was all about. He was sure they must know that Dougie MacClain had been a Watcher, and that was why he had been killed: because he had been trying to protect the hidden book. If that was the case, then Jake and Lauren would need the knowledge these kids were sure to have if they were to stop the Russians, and get the book for themselves. He took a deep breath, then stepped outside, into the paved area at the back of the house. Rona and Robbie were sitting on upturned crates, and they looked at him suspiciously. He could see that Rona had been crying.

'I'm so sorry about what happened to your uncle,' said Jake.

'He didn't fall!' burst out Rona angrily.

'Ssh, Rona,' said Robbie warningly.

'He didn't!' insisted Rona, and Jake could see the tears still shining angrily in her eyes. 'He knew every inch of those cliffs. He was pushed!'

'Rona!' snapped Robbie, firmer this time, and he shot an angry warning look at Jake.

'I understand,' Jake nodded sympathetically. And then he added in a quiet voice: 'He was a Watcher, wasn't he?'

For a split second both Robbie and Rona gaped at him, shock clearly shown on their faces. And then Robbie stood up, his face grim and hard.

'Are you saying he was some kind of peeping Tom?' he demanded angrily. And he advanced towards Jake, his fists clenched.

'I'm talking about the hidden books of Malichea,' said Jake softly.

Robbie stopped, and now he looked bewildered. Then he recovered himself.

'I don't know what you're talking about,' he muttered gruffly.

'But your sister does,' said Jake gently, turning towards Rona.

'You leave her alone!' shouted Robbie, and this time his fists came up, ready to throw a punch at Jake.

'You can attack me, but it doesn't alter the fact that your uncle was a Watcher whose job was to protect the book that's hidden here and stop it being dug up. My guess is, he tried to stop it in some way, and someone caught him and killed him.'

'The Russians!' sobbed Rona. 'They did it! But we can't prove it. And no one can touch them because they've got diplomatic immunity.' And she began crying again.

Robbie looked at his sister, his whole body language showing he was uncomfortable with all this.

'You shouldn't be saying this, Rona,' he said awkwardly.

'Why not?' demanded Rona, suddenly looking up, her eyes blazing angrily. 'He knows about the book. And Uncle Dougie's dead, and being silent isn't going to bring him back!'

Suddenly the realisation hit Jake, and he said: 'You're Watchers as well!'

Robbie looked at Jake in alarm, but Rona's look continued to be angry and defiant.

'Yes, we are! And proud of it!' she said.

Robbie still looked uncomfortable.

'How did you know?' he demanded.

'Because being a Watcher is handed down through generations, and your uncle didn't have children of his own, so it makes sense for it to be passed on to you.'

Robbie regarded Jake suspiciously.

'Are you a Watcher?' he asked.

'No,' said Jake, shaking his head. 'But I know a Watcher down south. She told me.'

'She wasn't supposed to,' said Robbie.

'She said I was in danger,' explained Jake. 'She did it to save my life.' Then he added with a slightly embarrassed smile. 'She thought I was one of the good guys.'

'And are you?' demanded Rona. 'One of the good guys?'

'I think I am,' said Jake. 'That's why we're here. To stop the Russians getting hold of the book.'

Inside he felt guilty because he didn't add the whole truth, that he and Lauren still wanted the book to bring the whole business of the hidden library out into the open. But if he told them that, they'd close up against him.

'How do we know we can trust you?' asked Robbie, still wary.

'You don't,' admitted Jake. 'But I've told you why

70

we're here, and that we know about the hidden books of Malichea.'

'So?' challenged Robbie. 'You could be working for someone else who wants the book.'

'True.' Jake nodded. 'But you can check me out with your senior Watchers. They'll tell you that I'm definitely not working for anyone with bad intentions.' Changing tack, he asked: 'Do your parents know about you two being Watchers?'

'Of course,' said Rona. 'It's in the family. They were pleased we decided to carry it on.'

'But we failed,' said Robbie bitterly.

'No we haven't,' said Rona fiercely. 'The Russians haven't found it yet!'

'But you two know where it is,' said Jake.

This time, the brother and sister looked at one another cautiously, then Rona said warily, 'We don't know you.'

They were interrupted by Mrs MacClain calling from inside: 'Robbie! Rona! Where are you?'

'We have to go,' said Robbie. He touched his sister on the shoulder. 'You OK?' he asked.

Rona nodded and stood up, wiping her eyes and her face with her sleeve.

'I'll be fine,' she said. She turned to Jake. 'Maybe we'll talk to you later.'

'I hope so,' said Jake.

Chapter 11

Jake went back into the guest house. He headed towards the lounge, but saw the door was shut and a handwritten notice had been stuck to it saying: *Private*. He wondered if Lauren was still in there, being questioned. Then he heard her voice from behind him call out, 'Jake!'

He turned and saw that she had just come downstairs.

'Where have you been?' she asked.

'Talking to Robbie and Rona,' said Jake. He told her about their conversation. When he finished, he could see that Lauren wasn't happy.

'You lied to them,' she said accusingly.

'No I didn't,' he defended himself. 'I just didn't tell them the whole story.'

'You didn't tell them that we plan to use the book to tell the world about the Order of Malichea,' said

Lauren. 'And that's exactly what the Watchers were set up to stop. Their job is to keep the books hidden.'

'Until the time is right for the information to come out,' countered Jake. 'Maybe *now* is the right time?'

Lauren didn't appear convinced.

'You lied to them,' she repeated. 'You led them to believe that we want the books kept hidden, the same way they do.'

'I was trying to get them on our side,' protested Jake.

'By lying to them,' insisted Lauren. 'If we go down that road, we'll be as bad as Pierce Randall. Pretending to be one thing, all public-spirited, but in reality wanting the books for our own ends.'

'Well, it may look that way . . .' began Jake defensively.

'It doesn't just look that way, it *is* that way,' Lauren told him firmly. She sighed. 'We have to forget this one.'

'What?' exploded Jake.

'We know there'll be other books,' said Lauren. 'We've already had our hands on two.'

'And lost both of them!' said Jake bitterly.

'Ask yourself: what's this one about? How to create spontaneous human combustion! How many people's lives will this science save?' She shook her head. 'No, we have to let this one go.'

'Why?' demanded Jake. 'You've come halfway around the world! You've put your whole life and liberty at risk to do what — abandon the search?'

'Just for this one,' said Lauren. 'I'm not going to get what we want by lying to them. Especially after what's happened to them, with their uncle being killed. We'll be taking advantage of their grief. I can't do that.'

The atmosphere at the guest house was one of gloom and mourning. The MacClains had disappeared to their own quarters, and no one felt like calling on them for anything.

Jake and Lauren wandered out to the garden, and found the Gordons sitting on one of the benches. Lauren and Jake joined them. The Gordons in particular looked deeply shocked by what had happened.

'How awful!' said Pam Gordon. She cast a look towards the house, and the annex where the family lived.

'I wonder if we ought to leave?' murmured John Gordon. 'After all, they won't feel much like running their guest house after this has happened.'

'I think they'll need our support,' said Lauren. 'And being busy can be a help at a time like this. Help dull the pain.'

The sound of footsteps approaching made them turn,

and they saw Ian Muir coming towards them, limping slightly. He pulled a chair over and joined them.

'I've just been answering questions from the police,' he said. He shook his head. 'Not that I could tell them much. Yes, I was out for a walk, but I didn't see him, or what happened to him.'

'Did the police give any clue as to what they think happened?' asked John Gordon.

Muir nodded.

'They seem to think it was an accident,' said Muir. 'He fell off the cliff.'

Mr and Mrs Gordon exchanged looks that showed their doubt about this.

'You don't think so?' asked Muir.

Mrs Gordon shrugged.

'Who knows?' she said. 'It just seems odd that someone who's spent their whole life around these cliffs should fall off them so easily.'

'That's often the way,' said Muir. 'People get complacent. That's the way accidents happen.' He turned to Jake and Lauren. 'What do you two think? You're the ones who found the body.'

Jake sighed.

'We just found him,' he said. 'He was a mess. His head was covered in blood. The police say it was hitting his head that killed him.'

'Which is odd,' said Mr Gordon. 'You'd have thought

he would have landed feet first and broken his legs, or something.'

'Maybe he tripped,' said Muir. 'Fell over and went down head first. Like I say, these things happen.'

'Perhaps the Russians might be able to throw some light on it,' said Pam Gordon. 'The place he was found isn't too far from their cottage.'

'That's what I said,' Muir told them. 'But it seems the Russians aren't able to help. Or, rather . . .' and he scowled, '. . . won't help.'

Jake frowned.

'What do you mean?'

'Apparently, they refuse to be questioned without their ambassador present, and it's going to take some time for her to arrive.'

'They can't refuse, surely?' asked Pam.

'It seems they're claiming diplomatic immunity,' said Muir.

'The police told you this?' queried Lauren. 'Isn't that a bit unusual for them to reveal things like that?'

Muir looked awkward.

'Yeah, well, they didn't exactly volunteer it,' he said. 'It sort of came out.'

He looked at the four, who were looking at him quizzically.

'OK,' he said. 'If you must know, they started getting heavy with me, so I told them if they carried on like that I was going to be claiming diplomatic immunity. And this cop groans "Just like the Russians!" That's when the story came out.'

'How can you claim diplomatic immunity?' asked Jake.

'I work for the State Department,' replied Muir. He shrugged. 'Nothing grand, just an ordinary desk job, but it gives me diplomatic status. Which can be useful in some situations.'

I bet, thought Jake.

Muir got up.

'Anyway, I'd better go phone my office back home, just in case these cops start checking up on me. See you guys later!'

With that he limped back towards the guest house.

'Well well,' said John Gordon. 'Diplomatic immunity. Who'd have thought it!' He turned to Lauren and smiled. 'Maybe you ought to try the same stunt: being a New Zealander and that. A foreign national.'

'It's too late for that.' Lauren smiled ruefully. 'They've already questioned me.'

Later, alone in their room, Lauren asked, 'What did you make of that?'

'Muir and his diplomatic immunity?' asked Jake. 'If you ask me, that definitely means he's CIA.'

'I was thinking of Mr Gordon,' said Lauren

thoughtfully. 'I never mentioned to the Gordons or Ian Muir that I'm from New Zealand. And my accent certainly doesn't sound like a Kiwi's.'

'Maybe the MacClains told them,' suggested Jake. 'I'm guessing you did the booking by email from New Zealand?'

'Yes.' Lauren nodded. 'Like I told you, I used Helen's computer.' She frowned. 'The MacClains *may* have told them, or maybe the Gordons are very nosy people who've been doing some serious checking on me.'

'Not too serious, let's hope,' said Jake, concerned. It was his turn to frown. 'I'm beginning to think that no one on this island is who or what they say they are.' He looked at Lauren. 'Do *you* think that Dougie's death was an accident?'

'No,' said Lauren. 'I think he was killed. And I think it was because of the hidden book.' She shuddered. 'Which means all of us who are here for it are at risk.'

Jake nodded.

'So the question is: which of us is next?'

Chapter 12

In the morning the guest house seemed to be back to normal, at least as far as the practicalities were concerned, like cooked breakfasts and packed lunches. Jeannie and Alec MacClain did their best to put a brave face on the situation, but there was no mistaking the grief that hung over them.

Jake and Lauren took their packed lunches and rucksacks and binoculars and set off to the area where the Russians were still hard at work at their dig. They found a sheltered spot some distance from the 'Neolithic site', and set about pretending to do some serious wildlife-watching, making notes of the different birds and animals they observed in a notebook, just in case they were challenged by anyone. But mostly they took turns to keep their binoculars trained on the dig site, watching the Russians at work.

'We're not the only ones watching,' commented

Jake after an hour of constant observation. 'I've just seen flashes of light reflected on some rocks on the other side. Looks like binoculars to me.'

'The Gordons?' suggested Lauren. 'Ian Muir?'

'No idea,' admitted Jake. Suddenly some activity inside the wire fence caught his eye. 'Hello. Looks like someone's found something!'

Immediately, Lauren left her study of the distant sea and joined him, lying down next to him and training her binoculars on the site.

The tall figure of Professor Lemski, the shorter squat figure of Dmitri close behind him, was running over to where two of them were coming out of a trench. One of the archaeologists, a man, was holding something up and gesticulating with it. Lemski reached the man and pushed him backwards, down into the trench, and then jumped down into the hole. They saw the archaeologist try to get back to his feet, but Lemski pushed him down again, out of sight, very roughly.

'Did you see that?' said Jake.

'So much for Mr Friendly,' said Lauren. 'He's trying to make sure that no one catches sight of whatever it is that's just been found.'

'I saw it,' said Jake.

'So did I,' said Lauren.

Both of them had recognised the object in the man's hand as something small and rectangular, wrapped in some kind of dark leather. The Russians had found the book!

Lemski turned and called out something to Dmitri, who ran off to where the team's equipment was stacked. Dmitri returned to the professor, carrying what looked like a refrigerated cold bag. He handed it to the professor, who ducked down, lifted the lid, put something in, and then stood up and handed it back to Dmitri.

'That's definitely the book,' said Lauren.

'So what are we going to do about it?' asked Jake. 'Are we still going to forget about it? Leave it to the Russians?'

Lauren shook her head.

'No,' she said. 'We can't let the Russians keep it. They'll use it as a weapon.'

'Well, if we're going to try and snatch it off them, we're going to be up against some strong competition,' Jake pointed out. 'We know of at least two: MI5 and the CIA. I bet you there are others out there as well watching this. It isn't going to be easy.'

Lauren fell silent, thinking it over.

'We're going to need the help of the MacClains,' she said.

'They're not going to want to get involved,' said Jake. 'Not after what's just happened. They're still torn up over Dougie.'

'But the two kids are Watchers,' Lauren reminded him. 'And they'll want revenge for what happened to their uncle. Getting the book back from the Russians will be a good way towards that revenge.'

'And you still plan to let the kids keep the book if we get it back?'

Lauren nodded.

'Yes,' she said.

Jake shook his head.

'I still think that's a bad move,' he said.

Rona was the first one they saw when they got back to the guest house. She was working in the small vege- table garden, weeding. Lauren and Jake headed straight for her.

'The Russians have found the book,' said Jake.

Rona looked at them, shocked. Then she pulled out her mobile phone and made a call.

'They've found it,' she said urgently. She listened for a second, then said, 'Meet us at the cave.'

She put away her mobile, then said to Jake and Lauren, 'We need to talk where we can't be heard.'

She wiped the soil from her hands, and headed for the path that led along the cliffs. Jake and Lauren followed, descending yet another path that twisted and turned down the rocky face of the cliff to the shore. They walked along the beach until they saw the two upturned boats that Dougie and Robbie had been painting.

'There's a whole series of caves along here,' said Rona. 'Some can be seen, but Robbie and I like this one. It's got trees and bushes in front of it, so no one ever goes in except people who know it, which usually means just us.' She gestured towards a clump of bushes and small trees apparently growing out of the rocks at the bottom of the cliff. They followed the girl towards the undergrowth. When they got there, Rona pushed her way through a thick bush, and disappeared. Jake and Lauren pushed their way through after her, and found themselves in a very narrow fissure in the rocks, but one that seemed to go a long way in.

Robbie was sitting inside the cave, waiting for them. He stood up as they came in.

'Is it true?' he asked.

Jake and Lauren nodded.

'We saw them,' said Jake. 'They put it in a cool bag.'

Robbie slumped back down on to the rocks, his head hanging down.

'We failed,' he said miserably. 'Our job was to stop the book from being found, and we failed!'

'It wasn't your fault,' said Lauren firmly. 'There was nothing you and your uncle could do against them.'

'That book has been hidden there for over thirteen

hundred years, kept safe by generations of Watchers, and we were the ones who lost it!'

'No,' said Lauren. 'The Russians had something that no one else who was looking for it had. They had The Index telling them where it was buried.'

Rona shook her head.

'They only had a fragment of The Index,' she said. 'I saw it.' She let out a deep sigh. 'Enough to spot what it was.'

She took out her mobile phone, then scrolled through various messages and pictures, until she came to a particular one and held it out towards Jake and Lauren.

'I was in the cottage soon after the Russians first arrived,' she said. 'I saw this photocopy of a part of a page on the table.'

Jake and Lauren studied the image. It was in an unfamiliar script.

'What language is this?' asked Lauren.

'Gaelic,' said Robbie. 'Goidelic Gaelic. The old style. We do it at school here.'

'That's what set alarm bells ringing,' said Rona.

'Can you translate it?' asked Jake.

Rona nodded.

'It says, "137. Dioscorides. *De Materia Medica Continuum*. Human Fire. Dalnaha."'

'Dalnaha is the name of this area of land, on the south side of Loch Spelve,' added Robbie.

84

'And the book the Russians have found is this one by Dioscorides, about spontaneous human combustion,' said Lauren.

'None of us knew what the book was about, just that it had to stay hidden,' said Robbie.

'How come you were in the cottage?' Jake asked Rona.

'A woman called Mrs Strange owns it,' replied Rona. 'She lives in Edinburgh and rents it out as a holiday let. Mum used to work for her, cleaning it and getting it ready for visitors. I used to help.' Her face darkened. 'Until the Russians arrived. They decided they would look after their own cleaning.'

'You look like there was more to it than that,' said Lauren gently. 'What happened?'

'It was the second week they were here,' said Rona. 'Mum and I had gone along to do the cleaning as usual, thinking Mrs Strange still wanted us to do the work for her. Mum has a key that Mrs Strange left with her. We were working away, when the Russians came back and found us, and one of them went ballistic, started shouting at us in Russian, and grabbed me by the arm and started shoving me towards the door. Mum stepped in and told him off for grabbing me, and I thought there was going to be a fight between them. But then that professor guy stepped in. The tall one.'

'Professor Lemski,' murmured Jake.

85

'That's him,' nodded Rona. 'He calmed things down, and ordered the other one out of the room. He apologised to Mum and me for his behaviour, and said our services wouldn't be needed as they would be looking after themselves. He was very nice about it, but there was something not quite right about him. Something . . .'

'Sinister?' suggested Lauren.

Rona nodded. 'He seems the friendly one, but don't get the wrong idea. He's the really tough one. The one in charge.'

Robbie sighed heavily.

'They'll be taking the book back to Russia,' he groaned.

'Not immediately,' said Jake. 'Like you say, I get the impression that this Professor Lemski is the one in charge, and he's not going to let it out of his hands. He'll hold on to it until he's ready to go. Which might give us a couple of days.'

'To do what?' asked Rona.

'Get the book back from them,' said Lauren.

'And then what?' asked Robbie sourly.

'You hide it again, somewhere else on Mull.'

Rona and Robbie stared at Lauren, disbelieving.

'You're not serious!' said Robbie.

'Yes, she is,' said Jake.

Robbie shook his head.

'You're mad,' he snorted derisively. 'If we hide it again, the Russians will know it was us who did it. They'll just grab us and make us tell them where it is.'

'How will they know it was you?' asked Lauren.

'Because if they know about the book, then they know about the Order of Malichea, which means they also know about the Watchers,' said Robbie. 'Which is why they killed Uncle Dougie. Which means they will have guessed that Rona and I are also Watchers. And if the book disappears, and they don't know where it's gone or who's taken it, they're bound to suspect us first. And they'll torture us until we tell them where we've hidden it.'

He spoke slowly, but bitterly, as if he was explaining something very simple to a pair of idiots.

Which we are, thought Jake. What Robbie said made perfect sense. Unless . . .

'Unless we fool them into thinking that someone else has got it,' he said.

Robbie and Rona looked at him enquiringly.

'How?' asked Robbie challengingly.

'MI5!'

'MI5?' Rona echoed.

Jake nodded.

'MI5 want to keep the Malichea books secret as well. On the few occasions that one of the books has surfaced, MI5 have done their best to get hold of it and hide it away in a vault so that no one can get their hands on it.'

Robbie shook his head.

'None of the books in the Highlands and islands have been found,' he told them.

'You don't know that for sure,' Lauren pointed out. 'You only guard your own book. Who's to say that a book somewhere else, maybe hidden on Barra, or Skye, or anywhere else hasn't been found in the past. That's certainly been the case with the books that were hidden from the library of Malichea at Glastonbury.'

Robbie and Rona fell silent, then Rona admitted awkwardly, 'I suppose it's possible.'

'The point is, we're sure that MI5 already know about what's going on here. They'll be desperate to get their hands on the book and get it away from the Russians.'

'So why don't they just do that?' asked Robbie. 'They've got the power.'

'International politics,' explained Lauren. 'If MI5 snatched the book, it could cause a big political row with the Russians. And right now the country depends on the Russians for gas supplies. The last thing the government wants is the Russians cutting off our gas, or trebling the price we pay for it.'

'But if we take it from the Russians and let them believe that MI5 have got it, you'll be off the hook,' said Jake.

'But how do we persuade the Russians that MI5 have got the book?' asked Rona.

'We get hold of the book and tell MI5 we'll give it to them if they agree to our demands,' said Jake. 'But instead of giving it to them, we make up a fake book. We arrange a high-profile handover, where we make sure the Russians see the book being handed over to MI5. In the meantime, we give you two the real book, and you hide it again. Somewhere here on Mull, where only you two know.

'Once that's done, the Russians will assume that MI5 have got the book, so it's not worth looking for it any longer, and they'll go home.'

'It won't work,' said Rona. 'Even if you get it off the Russians, MI5 will know it's a fake. They'll throw you both in jail.'

'Yes, well, that's the difficult part,' admitted Jake. 'That, and getting the real book off the Russians.'

They fell silent, a heavy gloomy silence. Jake was the first to speak. 'OK, has anyone got any other ideas?'

It was Rona who answered him: 'If we can get the book back, we let MI5 have it. Properly. Not pretending.'

Robbie stared at her, shocked.

'What?' he demanded.

'We know it's true what they say: that MI5 want to keep the books secret as well. Well, this way the book will still be hidden.'

'No!' burst out Robbie angrily. 'The books were supposed to stay hidden where no one can touch them. If any government has them, even stashed away somewhere, one day they might decide to use the information in them. That's why the Watchers were set up. And we are Watchers!'

'The book's already been found!' Rona reminded him firmly. 'We're watching over nothing! The only question now is who we want it to stay with: the Russians, who killed Uncle Dougie and will use it to make dreadful weapons; or British intelligence, who'll keep it hidden away.'

'No!' repeated Robbie furiously. He stood up and glared at them. 'I won't listen to any more of this! I'm going to get that book back! I'll destroy it rather than let anyone get their hands on it!'

'As Rona said, the Russians already have their hands on it,' said Jake.

'Not for long!' snapped Robbie. 'Come on, Rona!'

Rona shook her head.

'Not just yet,' she said. 'I want to talk about this some more.'

'There's nothing more to say!' said Robbie angrily. 'We're finished! We're on our own!'

'Not if we want justice for Uncle Dougie,' said Rona.

Robbie hesitated, and Jake could tell he was on the point of another angry outburst. But then he checked himself.

'Very well,' he said. 'But if you decide to work with them, that's nothing to do with me.'

With that, he turned and stormed off.

'I'm sorry,' Rona apologised. 'Robbie's really upset by what happened to Uncle Dougie. They were really close. And he takes his responsibility as a Watcher very seriously.'

'We understand,' said Lauren sympathetically. 'And we'd also understand if you take the same view as him. About recovering the book yourselves and destroying it.'

Rona shook her head.

'It won't work for all the reasons we said. If we take it, the Russians will know it was us and they'll make us tell them what we've done with it. And what's the point of destroying it? The science in the book was meant to be used some day. Destroying it would be a terrible thing to do.'

'OK,' said Lauren. 'So we're agreed, the first thing to do is get the book from the Russians. Which means finding out where they'll be keeping it.'

'We think they'll take it to the cottage,' said Jake. 'They won't leave it at the site. The problem is, the cottage is heavily guarded. And it'll be even more so once the book's there.'

Rona fell silent, thinking. Then she said, 'There's a secret way in.'

Jake and Lauren looked at her, intrigued.

'Where?' asked Jake.

'There's a tunnel that goes up from one of the caves on the shore, and comes out at the back of a cupboard in the kitchen. It was used by smugglers, getting stuff in and out of boats without being seen.

'Robbie and I watched when Mrs Strange had the cottage done up by Glenmorie the builders, so we know they left that secret entrance intact.'

'Maybe the Russians have discovered it?' suggested Lauren.

Rona shook her head.

'Unlikely,' she told them. 'You can only really find it from the tunnel side.'

'So, that's our way into the cottage,' said Jake.

'Unless Robbie goes in that way before us,' mused Lauren.

'Leave him to me,' said Rona. 'I'll talk to him, get him to hold off.'

'And if he doesn't?' asked Jake.

'I think you'd better show us this cave, Rona,' said Lauren. 'The sooner we get in and grab the book, the better.'

Chapter 13

The cave with the entrance to the secret tunnel was a further two miles along the shore. At first sight, it just looked like any ordinary cave: a narrow crevice in the cliff face with rocks around the entrance. Inside, though, there was a tunnel that twisted and turned, and finally came to what seemed to be a dead end, a blank wall of rock encrusted with barnacles. As they got nearer, Jake realised that the lower section of this apparent 'blank rock wall' was actually made of wood: ships' timbers fixed together. The rocks in the floor of the tunnel were wet and slippery, as had been the cave entrance.

'You can only get to it at low tide,' explained Rona. She indicated the barnacle-encrusted timber. 'I'm going to need help,' she said.

Jake and Lauren joined her, and the three of them working together pushed the timber to one side, and revealed a small opening. It was obvious that the piece of timber hadn't been moved in a very long time.

Rona pulled a small torch from her pocket, switched it on, and crawled through the opening, which was a long low tunnel. Jake and Lauren followed her. At the end, they came out into a much bigger cave, one high enough for them to be able to stand up in.

'There,' said Rona, pointing the torch to one side of the cave.

Jake and Lauren looked, and saw that a series of steps had been cut into the rock, disappearing upwards into another tunnel.

'It goes up and comes out at the back of a store cupboard in the kitchen,' said Rona.

'Right,' said Jake. He looked at Lauren. 'You up for this?' he asked.

'Of course,' said Lauren.

'I'll help as well,' said Rona.

Jake and Lauren exchanged doubtful looks.

'These people are dangerous,' said Jake. 'Remember what happened to your uncle.'

'I am a Watcher,' Rona reminded them firmly. 'It's my job.'

Jake saw Lauren hesitate, then she said to Rona, 'OK.'

Rona shone her torch on her watch.

'We'd better be getting back,' she said. 'Have a word with Robbie before he starts doing anything silly.'

They crawled back through the low tunnel, pushed the timber cover back into place over the entrance to the inner cave, and then made their way out into the sunlight again.

'It must have been hard work being a smuggler,' commented Jake, wiping the rock dust and wet sand off his clothes.

The sound of Rona's mobile ringing startled them. Rona checked the number. 'It's Mum,' she said. She clicked on, and listened for a few moments, then said, 'Yes, they're with me. I'll tell her. Thanks, Mum.'

She hung up, and Jake could tell it was bad news.

'Robbie?' he asked.

Rona shook her head.

'Some people from the Department of Immigration have just arrived,' she said. She turned to Lauren. 'They're looking for you.'

Jake and Lauren looked at one another, shocked.

'They know!' said Jake.

'Know what?' asked Rona.

Lauren hesitated, then she said, 'I'm here illegally.'

Rona laughed.

'You and half the workers in Glasgow and Edinburgh,' she said.

'No, I mean *really* illegally,' said Lauren. 'I was sent into exile in New Zealand.'

'Why?' asked Rona.

'Because of the books,' said Lauren. 'The ones from the Order of Malichea.'

'We found one,' added Jake. 'We lost it. The government took it off us, and they sent Laur . . . Helen away to stop us finding any more.'

Rona turned to Lauren.

'He called you Laur,' she said.

Lauren nodded.

'My real name. Lauren.'

'Lauren Cooper?'

Lauren shook her head.

'No,' she said. 'But it won't be fair to tell you more about me, otherwise you could be charged with being an accomplice. The less you know, the better for you.'

'What will happen to you now? With the Immigration people?'

'If I'm lucky, they'll send me back to New Zealand,' said Lauren.

'If she's not, she'll go to jail on some false charge,' said Jake with a groan.

'You can't go back,' said Rona. 'Not just yet. We need to work out how to get you off the island. Until then, you're going to have to hide somewhere.'

'In the cave?' suggested Jake, pointing at the cave they'd just come out of.

'No.' Rona shook her head. 'There's always a chance you might be found. The best place would be Uncle

Dougie's boat shed. It's got a lock on it and you'll be comfortable there.' She patted her pocket. 'I've got a key. So has Robbie.' She smiled. 'Uncle Dougie let us use it as a hidey-hole.'

'Is that the place near where Dougie was painting his boats?' asked Jake.

'That's the one.' Rona nodded. 'No one ever goes in it. You should be safe there until we can get you away.'

'Thank you,' said Lauren.

Rona smiled.

'It looks like we're all in this together,' she said. 'So we've got to help one another.'

'I'd better get back to the guest house and keep these people talking, while you two go off to the hut,' said Jake. 'We don't want them roaming around the island looking for you until Rona's got you safely hidden.'

Rona looked troubled.

'So much happening,' she said. 'Uncle Dougie killed. Immigration looking for you. Are these books worth it?'

'Oh yes,' said Lauren firmly. 'They really are.'

Chapter 14

A man and a woman were waiting in reception as Jake walked in through the main door of the guest house. They headed towards Jake as he made for the stairs.

'Mr Jacob Wells?' asked the man.

'Yes,' said Jake.

The man produced what looked like a warrant card.

'Hector Manvers, Department of Immigration,' he announced. 'This is my colleague, Susan Webb.'

'Nice to meet you,' said Jake. He frowned. 'Immigration? I can't see how that affects me. I was born in the UK.'

'We're not here to see you, but your companion,' said Webb. 'The woman who calls herself Helen Cooper.'

Jake stared at them, doing his best to look incredulous.

'Calls herself?' he repeated, sounding bewildered. Then he laughed. 'Yes, in the same way that you call yourself Susan Webb.'

'Could you tell us where she is?' asked Manvers.

'Here, I hope,' said Jake. 'Upstairs, in our room.'

'She isn't,' said Manvers.

Jake frowned.

'That's strange,' he said. 'She said she wanted to get back, so she left before I did. I wanted to stay and look at the view a little longer.'

'Did she say why she wanted to come back before you did?' asked Webb.

'She said she wanted to write some postcards for friends back home,' said Jake. 'She's from New Zealand.'

Manvers studied Jake, suspicion written all over his face.

'Is that what she says?' he asked.

'That's what she says, and that's what her passport says,' countered Jake.

'Oh, you checked her passport, did you?' asked Webb quickly.

Damn, thought Jake. Don't give them too much information, he warned himself.

'No,' said Jake. 'We showed each other our passports to have a laugh at our photographs. Have you ever seen a passport photograph that didn't make anyone look a complete idiot?' He studied the pair of them back. 'Mind, in your job, I suppose you see a lot of passports.'

'Where exactly did you leave the woman calling herself Helen Cooper?' asked Webb.

'Look, will you stop describing her as "the woman calling herself Helen Cooper"!' snapped Jake irritably.

'Where did you leave her?' pressed Webb.

'I didn't leave her at all,' said Jake. 'I told you, she left first.'

'Where from?' demanded Manvers.

'Out on the cliffs, near the loch,' said Jake.

Manvers and Webb exchanged looks, then Manvers nodded and said, 'We may need to talk to you again.'

'Well, I'm not going anywhere,' said Jake. 'Anyway, what's all this about? What do Immigration want with Helen?'

'We'll tell you that after we've discussed it with Miss Cooper,' said Manvers.

'Yes, well, right now I'm a bit worried about her,' Jake told them. 'She should have been back here by now.' He headed for the main door. 'I'm going to see if I can find out what's happened to her.'

Manvers moved quickly, joining Jake as he reached the door.

'It might be a good idea if I came with you,' he said. 'Just in case there's been an accident.'

'Yes.' Jake nodded. 'Good idea. What about your colleague?'

'She'll stay here, in case Miss Cooper returns while we're away.'

'Fine,' said Jake. 'Let's go.'

Jake walked out of the guest house, followed by Manvers. He headed along the cliff path towards the dig, and the cottage where the Russians were staying, keeping away from the shore and the path down to the boat hut. After his slip about the passport, Jake decided his best course of action was to say nothing; just respond when Manvers asked a question. But Manvers turned out to be a dour and reticent type, giving nothing away. As a result, their walk along the cliff path was done in silence. Jake used the walk to scan around the area, pretending to be searching for any sign of Lauren. Manvers, for his part, kept his attention on Jake. He obviously didn't believe that Lauren, or 'Helen Cooper', was going to be found anywhere on this walk.

He's too clever by half, thought Jake warily.

As they neared the wire fence surrounding the dig, Jake gestured towards it.

'I'm surprised you're not taking a look at those Russians,' said Jake. 'I would have thought that was more valid than coming all this way just to check on Helen.'

101

'All the people involved in the dig have Russian passports and valid visas,' said Manvers curtly. 'We've checked.'

They continued walking until they reached the far headland. Jake turned to look at Manvers, doing his best to put on a worried expression.

'I don't understand this,' he said. 'We should have seen her by now.'

'Are you sure she was here?' asked Manvers.

'Of course I'm sure!' said Jake. 'There aren't that many places around here!' He went to the edge of the cliff and looked down. 'This is where Dougie MacClain was found,' he muttered.

'I understand it was you and Miss Cooper who found the body,' said Manvers.

'Yes.' Jake gestured down to the shore. 'With that happening, you can understand why I'm worried about Helen.'

'You think she might have fallen off the cliff?' asked Manvers. 'Couldn't she have gone for a walk in some other direction?'

'If that was the case, why did she head off back to the guest house first?' demanded Jake.

Manvers' face remained impassive.

'I don't know,' he said coldly. 'You tell me.'

'I can't!' exploded Jake. He turned inland and looked at the expanse of heath and heather. 'She could have fallen down a crag or something. She could be lying somewhere helpless!'

'In that case I think it would be a good idea to call in search and rescue,' said Manvers calmly. 'Do a thorough search of the area.'

Which would mean looking in every small outbuilding, realised Jake. Including Dougie MacClain's boat hut. But hopefully he'd be able to get a message to Lauren to give her time to get away from there and hide somewhere else. Perhaps in the secret tunnel up to the cottage where the Russians were staying.

'Yes.' Jake nodded. 'That's what we have to do.' He turned and set off back the way they'd come. 'I'll talk to Alec MacClain. He'll set things in motion.'

The walk back to the guest house was at a much faster pace than the walk out, Jake made sure of that, determined to show the urgency he felt about getting the search for 'Helen Cooper' under way. He could tell, however, that Manvers didn't seem impressed. The Immigration officer remained silent all the way back.

Susan Webb was standing outside in the parking area as they returned, and Manvers broke away from Jake and went to her. They put their heads together and engaged in a whispered conversation, and then the two of them went off again but in a different direction.

Jake felt a bolt of fear. Had Webb found something out? Had she discovered where Lauren was hiding?

As Jake entered the guest house, he ran into Alec and Jeannie MacClain. The worried-looking couple had obviously been waiting for him.

'Can I have a word with you, Mr Wells?' asked Alec MacClain.

'Of course,' said Jake.

'Outside would be best,' Alec MacClain added. 'Less chance of being overheard.'

Jake followed them through the guest house, and out the back door into the rear garden. It was obvious that both were under stress. Jeannie MacClain, in particular, looked very strained. Alec followed them past the raised beds with vegetables to the compost bins, a good distance from the house. Alec turned to Jake, his expression grim.

'What are you up to with our children?' he demanded.

'Both Rona and Robbie have come back in strange moods,' said Jeannie. 'Robbie's angry and Rona . . . Well, Rona's suddenly very nervous and secretive.'

Jake hesitated. This was no time for lying, Alec and Jeannie would see through him easily. And the MacClains were already involved.

'It's about the hidden books,' said Jake. 'The Order of Malichea.'

Alec and Jeannie exchanged concerned looks.

'I know that your brother, Dougie, was a Watcher,' Jake continued. 'And that Rona and Robbie are too.'

'But that's over now,' said Jeannie. 'The Russians have got the book. Robbie told us.'

'It's not over,' said Jake, shaking his head. 'We plan to get the book back off the Russians.'

Jeannie frowned.

'Why have Immigration turned up?' she asked.

'I don't know,' admitted Jake. 'It's all a bit too much of a coincidence, if you ask me . . .'

He was cut off by a scream, followed by a girl's voice from inside the house calling: 'Help! Help!'

'That's Rona!' said Alec MacClain, and he rushed towards the guest house, closely followed by Jeannie and Jake.

Robbie appeared from the side of the house, a look of concern on his face.

'What's happened?' he demanded.

But no one stopped to talk; Alec, Jeannie and Jake were running, into the house, then up the stairs to the first floor.

Rona stood at the end of the short corridor. There was blood on her dress. At her feet lay the body of a man.

'I thought he'd just fainted,' said Rona. 'Then I turned him over . . .'

Alec and Jake had gone to the body. It was John

Gordon, and his throat had been cut. Blood had gushed out and had soaked his clothes.

'Jeannie, get the ambulance and the police,' said Alec.

As he spoke, Jeannie was already halfway down the stairs, running to the phone at the reception desk.

First Dougie MacClain, now John Gordon, thought Jake.

'What's that in his hand?' asked Robbie.

They looked. A torn-off piece of material was clenched in Gordon's closed left fist. Robbie shot a suspicious look at Jake.

'That looks the same as your jacket,' he said.

Jake shook his head.

'There are loads of jackets made of the same material,' he said.

'Not here,' said Robbie. And suddenly he had snatched the key ring from his father's belt and was moving swiftly towards Jake's and Lauren's room.

'Hey!' called Jake.

'Robbie!' called Alec.

But Robbie had already unlocked the door of the room and rushed in. Jake hurried after him.

'Now look!' he protested. 'You can't just come in here and . . .'

Robbie had thrown open the wardrobe door and was rummaging through the clothes hanging up. With a cry of triumph he pulled a jacket from its hanger.

'There!' he yelled, brandishing it.

Jake looked at the jacket, stunned. There was a tear in the material, near the pocket.

And it'll match the one in Gordon's hand, thought Jake with a deep sick feeling. I'm being framed!

'Look, Dad!' said Robbie, holding the jacket towards his father, pointing at the place where the material had been torn from it.

'I didn't do it,' insisted Jake, turning to Alec MacClain. 'This is a set-up.'

'Oh yes?' demanded Robbie. His face showed a mixture of anger and triumph. Turning to his father, he said, 'I bet it was him who killed Dougie. Him and his girlfriend!'

'No!' protested Jake.

There was the sound of a woman giving an angry shout from downstairs, and then the pounding of feet up the stairs. They hurried out of the room to see Pam Gordon arriving at the top of the stairs. She stopped when she saw the dead body of her husband, and then moved purposefully towards him. Alec MacClain tried to step in her way, but she pushed him roughly aside. She knelt by the body, her face changing from pain to despair, and then deep deep anger, all in a few seconds.

'He did it!' shouted Robbie, pointing at Jake.

Pam Gordon turned and looked up at Jake, and the

107

hatred and anger in her eyes seared into him. If she could, she'd kill me right now, thought Jake.

'I didn't,' he said. 'It wasn't me!'

'We all ought to go downstairs and wait for the police,' said Alec MacClain.

'I'm staying here with him,' said Pam Gordon.

Her tone was flat and obstinate. There was no way she was going to be moved from John Gordon's body. Alec MacClain nodded, then he shepherded Jake, Rona and Robbie downstairs.

Chapter 15

Jake sat in the bar area, his mind in a whirl. Who had killed John Gordon? Someone who'd been able to get into his and Lauren's room and tear a piece off his jacket to plant in Gordon's hand. One of the MacClain family? They had the key to his room. No, Jake told himself dismissively. Not the MacClains. The Russians? But there had been no sign of any of the Russians around the guest house. But then a good assassin wouldn't be spotted. They'd creep in, do the kill, then creep out again. And they'd have the tools to open a simple lock.

What about Muir? Could it have been the American? He hadn't been seen since he left that morning for a ramble over the countryside; but that didn't mean he hadn't doubled back, killed Gordon, and then slipped away again, unseen.

He looked up as Alec MacClain came into the room.

'I didn't do it,' he said. 'Someone's trying to frame me. I don't know why, but they are.'

'The police are on their way,' said Alec.

Jake nodded. They'd arrest him on suspicion, he was sure of that. After all, the only piece of evidence pointed to him being the killer. His main concern was Lauren. He needed to get a message to her, tell her what had happened. But he couldn't leave the guest house, not until the police had been.

Rona would tell her, he was sure. But what about Robbie? Robbie was dead sure that it had been Jake who'd killed Gordon; and now he was starting to think that meant Jake had also killed Dougie. Which meant he'd think that Lauren was also involved. Would Robbie give Lauren away to the police? Or to Manvers and Webb?

He had to find a way to stop Robbie doing that, otherwise everything would be lost.

He looked at Alec MacClain, and then blurted out.

'Someone's trying to frame me. Me and Helen. Mostly they're after Helen.'

'The people from Immigration think she's an illegal immigrant,' said Alec.

'She's not,' said Jake. 'But she is . . .' He hesitated. 'At risk,' he finished.

'From what?' asked Alec.

'From someone who wants to get rid of her,' said Jake.

'Why?'

'Because of the books,' said Jake. 'The Malichea books.'

Alec frowned.

'Where is she?' he asked.

'Rona took her somewhere safe,' said Jake. 'But I'm worried that if Robbie says anything about where she is, she could end up like John Gordon. And your brother.'

Alec's expression hardened.

'Who's behind all this?' he asked. 'Dougie, and now Gordon?'

Jake sighed and shook his head.

'I don't know,' he said. 'All I'm asking is, can you stop Robbie giving Helen away to the authorities?'

'Why should I do that?' asked Alec.

'Because she knows more about the Order of Malichea and the hidden books than almost anyone else.'

'More than the Watchers like Dougie, and Robbie and Rona? More than the Russians?'

'Much more,' said Jake. 'That's why they're trying to get rid of her.'

He didn't know if it was actually true that Lauren knew more than the Russians, but she certainly knew more than everyone he knew. And he had to do something to try to keep her safe.

Alec studied Jake for a while, then he nodded.

'I'll have a word with Robbie,' he said.

'Thank you,' said Jake.

There was the sound of rushing feet, and then Manvers and Webb burst into the room. They were both out of breath.

'What's going on?' Manvers demanded. 'We were across the headland when we heard the sound of a siren. There's an ambulance and a police car and they look like they're coming here!'

'There's been an accident,' said Alec.

'A murder,' Jake corrected him.

They could hear the sirens getting nearer now.

Manvers threw a shocked look at Jake.

'Did you say murder?' he demanded.

'Yes,' said Jake. Suddenly a thought hit him. Were Manvers and Webb *really* from Immigration? Dougie MacClain had been battered to death, but Gordon's killing had been entirely different: his throat cut.

He was just about to say this thought aloud, when Jeannie MacClain came into the room.

'The police are here,' she said.

The ambulance crew had taken John Gordon's body away, and now the local police constable was questioning Jake. It was a very brief interview.

'I'm going to have to take you in for questioning,' the constable told Jake finally. 'That piece of cloth, you understand.'

Jake nodded, resigned.

'I didn't do it,' he said.

The constable nodded.

'I hear what you say, but I have to follow procedure.' He produced a pair of handcuffs. Jake looked at them, shocked.

'Are they really necessary?' he demanded.

'We're a small force on Mull,' said the constable. 'So it's just me taking you in. How would it look if you suddenly overpowered me on the journey and escaped?'

'But I'm innocent!' persisted Jake.

The constable nodded.

'I appreciate that, sir,' he said. 'But I have my job to do.'

Jake was about to raise more fervent objections, but he realised they would be of no use. The evidence was there, pointing to him as the suspect. The constable had to take him in.

'OK,' he said, and he held out his wrists for the cuffs.

All four MacClains, Pam Gordon, and Manvers and Webb, watched in silence as Jake was taken out of the guest house in handcuffs and put into the back of the small police van. The constable slammed and locked the rear doors shut. Jake sat down on the hard wooden bench that ran along the back of the van. The only windows in the back were two small wired-glass ones in the doors, and a tiny one between the rear of the van and the driver's compartment, also made of thick wired glass. So, no chance of escaping on the journey, thought Jake.

The van started up, and moved off.

I'm leaving Lauren behind, alone and on the run, thought Jake, feeling sick to his stomach. He hoped that Rona would tell her what had happened.

I'll come back for you, Lauren, he vowed. We've been in worse situations than this and survived them.

But, handcuffed as he was, heading away from the south of the island, he could feel that his words had a hollow ring to them. On an island, there really was nowhere to run.

Chapter 16

Once they reached the police station, Jake was put in a cell.

'Just until someone from CID arrives from the mainland,' the constable informed him, removing the handcuffs. He gave a rueful smile. 'Luckily for us, we don't need a regular detective presence on Mull. There's not that much crime.'

The door clanged shut, and Jake settled down to wait.

It took two hours for the detective to arrive. Or, at least, for Jake to be taken to the interview room where Detective Sergeant Stewart was sitting at a table waiting for him. Stewart was a calm-looking man in a rumpled brown jacket. He gestured for Jake to sit down, and the constable left the room to return to his duties guarding the reception desk.

'So, Mr Wells. Do you want to tell me what you are doing on Mull?' asked the detective.

'The same as I told your colleague before: I came to meet an old friend.'

Sergeant Stewart consulted the notes in front of him.

'Ah yes, this so-called Helen Cooper.'

'She is not the "so-called" Helen Cooper. She is Helen Cooper.'

'Not according to Mr Manvers of Immigration. He seems to think she's actually someone called Lauren Graham.'

'She's not.'

'Interestingly, when we tried to track down details about this Lauren Graham, we were referred to the intelligence services in London. Why would that be, do you think?'

'I've no idea.' Jake shrugged. 'Particularly as I've no idea who this Lauren Graham person you're talking about is.'

'That's interesting,' said Stewart, 'because their records show that once upon a time you shared an address in London with a Lauren Graham. Which Lauren Graham would that be?'

That would be the Lauren Graham I fell in love with, and who I moved in with for a whole month, before I messed things up and she kicked me out, thought Jake. Aloud, he said: 'That would be a girl I had a relationship with once, about a year ago. She is nothing to do with Helen Cooper.'

Stewart regarded him quizzically.

'Very well,' he said at last, 'we'll come back to that.'

'Have you found her yet?'

'Who?'

'Helen,' said Jake. 'She went missing just before you brought me up here.'

'Or did she disappear of her own volition?' asked Stewart.

'What do you mean?' asked Jake.

Suddenly Stewart's expression became hard, and Jake could see cold anger in his eyes as he looked directly into Jake's.

'I mean that for years — no, decades — we've had no major crime on Mull. And then you and this "Helen Cooper" arrive, and within a day Dougie MacClain is found dead. His body is found by you and this mysterious Helen Cooper, who later vanishes. Then another guest at the guest house where you are both staying is murdered. His throat's cut, and in his hand we find a piece of your clothing.'

'None of it is anything to do with me,' insisted Jake.

Stewart gave a sarcastic laugh.

'Oh, please!' he snorted.

'Shouldn't I have a lawyer?' asked Jake.

'We've arranged one for you,' said Stewart. 'He's coming from Oban. It'll take him a while to get here. Until then, we're just having an informal chat.'

'In that case I'll wait to say anything more until he gets here,' said Jake.

Stewart shrugged.

'As you wish,' he said.

He got up and went to the door, opened it and gestured to the uniformed constable standing outside.

'Put him back in the cell,' he said.

'On what charge?' demanded Jake.

'Suspicion of murder,' said Stewart.

As the cell door clanged shut on him for a second time, Jake's spirits sank even lower. He had to get out of here. He was no use to Lauren, sitting here in this cell. He wondered how she was. Was she safe, hiding in the boat hut? Or had Manvers and Webb found her? He wondered if the book was still on the island, or if the Russians had removed it already.

And he'd been framed for murder, and Lauren was on the run from immigration. What a mess! He groaned. Who had killed Gordon? He guessed it was the same people who had killed Dougie MacClain, and for the same reasons: to stop the opposition. It has to be the Russians, he thought. But there had been no sign of any of the Russians anywhere near the guest house when Gordon had been killed.

He sat in the cell for another half-hour, although it seemed much longer. Then the cell door opened and the constable looked in.

'OK, you,' he said. 'Out you come.'

'Has my lawyer arrived?' asked Jake.

'Something like that,' said the constable.

Jake stepped out of the cell and followed the constable, puzzled. 'Something like that.' What did that mean? Either his lawyer had arrived or he hadn't.

They walked into the main reception area of the police station, and Jake stopped. Pam Gordon was at the desk with Detective Sergeant Stewart, signing some papers. She signed the last of them and handed them all to Stewart.

'There you are,' she said.

'Thank you,' said Stewart. 'He's all yours.'

Pam Gordon gestured towards the door.

'My car's outside,' she told Jake.

Stunned by this sudden turn in events, Jake followed her out of the police station. What was going on? Why had Pam Gordon turned up? A sudden bolt of fear shot through Jake. She'd sprung him from jail to kill him in revenge for killing John Gordon! But that didn't make sense. What power did she have that could force Stewart to hand Jake over as easily as that? Of course, he and Lauren had suspected she was MI5. This proved it.

They got into the car, and then Jake blurted out: 'I didn't kill him.'

'If I thought you had, I'd have killed you before you even got in the car,' she said bluntly.

119

She started the ignition, and they moved off.

'Where are we going?' asked Jake.

'Back to Craigmount,' she said.

They headed along the road away from the coast and into the heart of the south part of the island.

'How did you manage it?' asked Jake. 'Getting me out of there, I mean.'

'I had authority,' said Gordon. 'Orders to follow.'

'Whose?' asked Jake.

'Let's just say an old boss of yours.'

'Not Gareth Findlay-Weston?'

Gareth Findlay-Weston, Jake's former boss when he worked as a trainee press officer at the Department of Science; and — beneath that cover of a bureaucratic desk job — a top figure in MI5.

Gordon glared at him.

'You do throw names around, don't you?' she snapped. 'God, you'd make a terrible agent!'

'We'd already guessed you were both MI5,' said Jake defensively. His voice softened as he said: 'I'm sorry about John.'

She shook her head.

'Whoever killed him must be good. A real professional. John would never have allowed an amateur to get that close to him. That's why I don't think it was you. Like I said, if I thought it was, you'd be dead by now.' She frowned. 'Although you may just be playing

120

a clever game and putting on the pretence of being enthusiastic amateurs. You and that girlfriend of yours. Lauren Graham.'

Jake threw a surprised look at her.

'You don't think we bought that story of her being someone called Helen Cooper, do you?' said Gordon scornfully. 'John clocked her as soon as he saw her. He's got a photographic memory for faces.' She corrected herself bitterly. 'Had.' She scowled, then said: 'We'd been told to watch out for you once we knew that the Russians were after the Malichea book. Your old boss was sure that you'd come looking for it. We got a bit of a surprise when Ms Graham turned up first.' She nodded admiringly. 'She's good, I'll give her that. Getting back to the UK like that, without getting stopped. Very impressive.'

'I suppose it was you who shopped her to Immigration,' said Jake.

'Not us,' said Gordon. 'We were told to leave you both in place. I think You Know Who thought you'd both be a good decoy. Take the Russian's attention away from us.'

'Do you have to call him You Know Who, and He Who Must Not Be Named?' asked Jake. 'It makes him sound like Lord Voldermort.'

For the first time, Jake saw a smile pass over Pam Gordon's face.

'You know, I think he'd like that,' she said. 'Very appropriate.' Then her face turned grim again. 'By the way, your girlfriend's disappeared.'

'Yes, we know,' said Jake. 'She disappeared before I was taken away.'

'No, I mean *really* disappeared,' said Gordon. 'She's gone from that boathouse place where she was hiding, and it looks like there was some kind of struggle.'

Jake let this sink in, horrified.

'Where is she?' he demanded.

'If we knew that, we'd be doing something about it,' said Gordon.

'It's got to be the Russians,' said Jake.

'Why?' asked Gordon. 'They've got the book. Why would they want to draw attention to themselves by kidnapping your girlfriend?'

'The same reason they killed Dougie MacClain,' said Jake. 'Because they know she wants to stop them keeping the book.'

'So what?' Gordon shrugged. 'They'd also know she doesn't pose much of a threat to them. Certainly not one worth bothering about.' Her face darkened again as she added, 'Unlike a top agent like John.'

'You think they killed John?' asked Jake.

Gordon scowled.

'I don't know,' she said. 'We're not even sure they killed Dougie MacClain.'

'If they didn't, who did?'

'We're not sure. Anyway, none of the Russians were anywhere around the guest house when John was killed.'

'What about Ian Muir?' asked Jake.

'What about him?'

'Is he CIA?'

'What makes you think that?'

'Well, he's American.'

Gordon let out a groan.

'God, you are so simplistic!'

'As the Russians were there, it made sense for the CIA to have a presence!' said Jake defensively.

'The CIA are in one of the holiday cottages along the lane,' Gordon said. 'Inside, it's bristling with high-tech satellite technology. There's no way they could fit all the equipment they need into a room in the guest house without anyone knowing.'

'So who's Muir working for?'

'We don't know,' admitted Gordon.

'Pierce Randall?' suggested Jake.

Gordon shot him a quick look.

'You've really got a bug about those guys, haven't you?' she said.

'Can you blame me?' asked Jake. 'They've been involved in anything to do with the Malichea books right from the word go.'

Gordon thought it over, and nodded.

'It's possible,' she said. 'But there's been no contact between Muir and Pierce Randall since he's been on the island.'

'How can you be so sure?'

'Because the CIA aren't the only ones with state-of-the-art surveillance equipment,' said Gordon.

They fell silent.

'So who's got Lauren?' asked Jake finally.

'We don't know,' admitted Gordon. She hesitated, then said: 'Maybe she's not on the island any longer.'

'What do you mean?'

Gordon hesitated again, then said: 'Look, these are dangerous people we're dealing with. Whether it's the Russians or someone else. Muir, maybe. Think what happened to Dougie MacClain and John. If your friend got too close to them . . .'

'No!' snapped Jake. 'I'd know if something had happened to her.'

'How?' asked Gordon. 'Telepathy between lovers?' She shook her head. 'I'm sorry, I don't buy it. It could be she was dealt with and dumped in the sea, far enough out for it to sink. The first we'll know about it is when the spring tides bring her body in.'

Jake shut his eyes to block out the image and shook his head violently.

'No!' he said again.

'You've got to admit, it's a possibility,' said Gordon. She sighed. 'Look, I shouldn't even be saying this. I was told to keep you on the hook, and that means you thinking that she's still out there somewhere, being kept prisoner, and you can ride to her rescue with our help.'

'Why would you do that?'

'For the book. Our people want you to get it for us.'

Jake let that sink in. Finally, he asked, 'Why me? Like you said, you're the professionals. I'm just an amateur.'

'Because He Who Shall Not Be Named seems to think you can get places we can't. He says you've done it before.' She gave a mirthless grin. 'If you want my opinion, he wants you to try because if you get caught then it doesn't come back on us.'

'And if they kill me?'

She fell silent, then she shrugged.

'What can I say? One more dead body, but nothing to do with MI5.'

Jake thought it over as Gordon continued driving. If he agreed, and was successful, then MI5 would get the book and hide it away, along with the others. Any chance he and Lauren might have of getting the information about the Order of Malichea into the public domain would be gone. And he'd be going in alone, Gareth wouldn't want to take the chance of the

Russians being able to put the body of a dead MI5 agent, caught while trying to steal 'Russian property', on display.

But there was still a chance that the Russians were holding Lauren prisoner, despite Gordon's doubts about that. He had to believe that Lauren was still alive, otherwise all of this would be for nothing.

'OK,' he said finally. 'I'll do it. But I want something in return.'

'We'll give you back-up, as much as we can without being seen to be involved,' nodded Gordon.

'I'm not talking about back-up,' said Jake. 'I want a deal. If I do this, then Gareth agrees to let Lauren back into the country, and any charges against her are dropped. Second, I want my old job back.'

Gordon laughed.

'You're mad!' she said. 'He's not going to go for either of those.'

'He will if he wants me to get the book back off the Russians,' said Jake. 'And I want his agreement in writing.'

Gordon fell silent. Then she said, 'You're serious, aren't you?'

'Deadly serious,' said Jake. 'I'm guessing that you've got one of those state-of-the-art phones that you can link to a printer.'

Gordon shrugged.

'I may have,' she said.

'And it'll have some kind of scrambler on it so you can send messages safely in code.'

Again, Gordon gave a small smile.

'You've been watching too many James Bond films,' she said.

'No,' he said. 'I've been put under surveillance before, and by experts.'

Chapter 17

As the car pulled up in front of their guest house, Jake saw Manvers and Webb putting their luggage into their car.

'Looks like someone's called the dogs off,' murmured Gordon.

'Or they don't think it's worth staying here now that Lauren's disappeared,' suggested Jake.

Gordon sighed.

'If you want my advice, you ought to carry on calling her Helen Cooper,' she said. 'When you get a cover story you have to stick to it.'

'But I'm only talking to you, and you know who she really is,' countered Jake.

'Yes, but you always have to assume you can be overheard,' said Gordon. 'Spy School Basic.'

Jake nodded.

'Point taken,' he said.

They waited until Manvers and Webb had driven off before they got out of Gordon's car, to avoid any awkward questions the Immigration inspectors might ask. But, from the grim expressions on the faces of Manvers and Webb, it didn't look as if they were much inclined to start a conversation anyway.

'I'll get on to Lord Voldemort for you,' said Gordon. 'Let's see what he says.'

They entered reception, and Gordon headed straight upstairs. Through the open door of the bar area, Jake saw Alec, Jeannie and Rona MacClain talking. Time to sort some things out and clear the air, he thought.

He walked into the bar. The three were so deeply engaged in their conversation, talking in low and urgent tones, that they weren't aware of Jake's presence at first, until Jeannie MacClain half turned and saw him.

'Mr Wells!' she said.

Immediately, Alec and Rona stopped talking and turned to look at him, startled.

'I'm sorry for all the trouble you've had,' said Jake apologetically, 'but it wasn't me who killed John Gordon.'

'No, that was the impression we got from Mrs Gordon,' said Alec. He frowned, puzzled. 'Though how she knew . . .' He shook his head. 'Especially as it was her husband who died.'

'I was framed,' said Jake. 'Someone wanted me out of the way. And John Gordon. And Helen. And Dougie.'

'Why?' asked Jeannie.

'The book,' said Rona.

'It has to be,' said Jake. 'It's the only thing that links us.' Desperately hoping for good news, he asked, 'Has there been any news of Helen?'

They shook their heads.

'What happened?' asked Jake.

'I went to the boat hut to take her some food,' said Rona. 'The door had been broken open and she was gone.'

'I went along when Rona called me,' added Alec. 'It looked like there'd been signs of a struggle. A chair was lying on its side, things had been pulled off the shelves.'

'Any car tracks?' asked Jake.

Alec shook his head.

'No,' he said.

'It has to be the Russians,' said Rona.

'Really?' queried Jake. 'Now they've found the book I'd have thought they'd be packing up.'

'It doesn't look like it,' said Alec. 'We've been taking turns to keep an eye on them. Soon after the book was found, two of the Russians took the ferry to the mainland.'

'Foot passengers?'

Alec shook his head.

'They took one of their cars.'

'Anyone we know? The professor? The one they call Dmitri?'

Again, Alec shook his head.

'No, just two of the so-called archaeologists. One of them speaks good English. I checked with a pal of mine on the ferry.'

'When did they go?'

'Yesterday afternoon.'

Jake thought over the implication of this.

'It sounds like they've been sent to get something.'

'If it was just supplies, they'd have been back by now,' said Alec.

'So it's something out of the ordinary.' Jake nodded. 'I think it's something to do with the book. Has Rona told you what the book is?'

'Something to do with spontaneous human combustion,' said Jeannie. She frowned. 'Why is that important enough for people to be killed over?'

'Because it's about how to make it happen,' said Jake.

'You mean, like a formula or a recipe?' asked Rona.

'Yes,' said Jake.

'So you think those two have gone to get the ingredients they need?' asked Jeannie. 'Somewhere they're more likely to get special stuff, like Glasgow, or Edinburgh?'

Jake sighed.

'I don't know,' he said. 'I'm just guessing. My feeling is that the professor wants to check that what's in the book works. If it doesn't, then it could mean that what they've found is only part of it, so there could be more of the book hidden here at the site. That's the only reason I can think of why they haven't started to leave.'

'If what you say is right, we ought to intercept those two Russians when they come back,' suggested Alec. 'Maybe we could get the police to search them and their car as soon as they arrive at Oban.'

'But we don't know what they'll be bringing back,' pointed out Jake. 'It could be some innocent-looking herbs.' He sighed, then asked, 'Where's Robbie?'

'He's working on Dougie's boats,' said Rona.

'He feels he needs to do it for Dougie's memory,' said Alec.

'And he wants to keep an eye on the Russians,' added Rona.

Jake nodded.

'Will it be all right with you if I go and have a word with him?' he asked Alec and Jeannie.

'Are you going to have a row with him about what he said?' asked Alec warily. 'About you killing John Gordon?'

Jake shook his head.

'No,' he said. 'I just want to try and make my peace

132

with him. The only way to find out what's happened to Helen is if we work together.'

'I don't want him getting in any deeper than he is,' warned Alec.

'I know,' said Jake. 'And I'll do my best to try and talk him out of doing anything silly.'

Jeannie sighed.

'We've tried to do that, but he's stubborn,' she said. 'Just like Dougie.'

'We thought about sending him away until this is over,' said Alec. 'He can stay with relatives on the mainland.'

'But he refuses to go,' said Jeannie unhappily. 'Said if we sent him away, he'd get a boat and sneak back.'

'He feels he's responsible,' said Rona. 'For the book being found.'

Jake nodded.

'I'll see what I can do,' he told them.

'He won't listen to you,' said Jeannie.

'No, I don't think he will,' said Jake. 'But at least I can try.'

Chapter 18

Robbie was sitting on a crate beside the two upturned boats. He turned as he heard Jake approach, and scowled.

'So they let you go,' he said sullenly.

'Because I'm innocent,' said Jake. 'I was framed.'

Robbie let out a snort of disbelief.

'Mrs Gordon herself came to bring me back,' said Jake. 'She wouldn't have done that if she thought I'd killed her husband.'

'There's something suspicious about her,' growled Robbie. 'I don't think she's who she says she is either. Like you!' he added accusingly.

Jake hesitated, then asked, 'Can we talk?'

'About what?' demanded Robbie.

He was angry. His beloved uncle had been killed and the book they'd both sworn to protect had been dug up.

'About the book,' said Jake. 'About finding Helen.'

'The Russians have got her,' said Robbie.

Jake's heart gave a leap.

'Do you know that for sure?' he asked. 'Have you seen her?'

'No,' said Robbie. 'But if she'd gone into the sea, her body would have been found by now. Either it would have come in with the tide, or one of the boats would have spotted something floating.'

Jake's feeling of hope sank into the pit of his stomach. For a second he'd thought that Robbie had caught sight of Lauren.

'We need to get the book back,' said Jake firmly.

'No,' said Robbie, glowering at Jake. '*I* need to get the book back so I can destroy it. You want it back so you can give it to MI5 or whoever.'

'It shouldn't be destroyed,' said Jake. 'The monks buried it so the information in it would be kept safe.'

'And now it isn't,' retorted Robbie. 'It's been found, and it's in the wrong hands.'

'If we work against each other, we could end up getting in each other's way,' Jake pointed out. 'We stand more chance of getting the book off the Russians if we work together.'

'And then what?' challenged Robbie. 'What do we do? Fight for it? See who wins?' He gave another snort of derision. 'You must think I'm an idiot!'

'No, I don't,' said Jake. 'I think you're angry, and with good reason. But I don't think it'll help get the book or Helen back.'

Jake gestured at a spare crate near one of the upturned boats.

'Mind if I sit down?' he asked.

'Why?' demanded Robbie. 'I've got nothing to say to you!'

'For one thing, there's the secret tunnel,' said Jake. 'Rona showed it to me.'

'That's no way in,' said Robbie, shaking his head.

Jake frowned, surprised.

'We saw it,' he said. 'It looks like the best way in. The *only* way in.'

'If the Russians have got your girlfriend, she'll have told them about it,' said Robbie.

'No she won't,' said Jake firmly.

'Are you prepared to stake your life on that?' asked Robbie. 'I'm not. They killed Uncle Dougie. They won't have any qualms about doing whatever it takes to make your girlfriend tell them everything she knows. And that includes telling them about the secret tunnel.'

At the thought of Lauren being interrogated — no, tortured — by the Russians Jake felt a sick feeling deep in his stomach.

'So how are you planning to get in?' he asked.

136

Once again, Robbie glowered at him.

'Wouldn't you like to know?' he grunted. 'I've got my own way to get in, and it's staying my way.'

Jake looked at the angry boy. There was so much he wanted to say to try to convince Robbie that they'd have more chance working together, but he could tell by the boy's manner that right now nothing he said would persuade him.

'OK,' said Jake. 'But if you change your mind . . .'

'I won't,' snapped Robbie curtly.

Jake nodded resignedly. Then he turned and headed back towards Craigmount.

As Jake walked across the forecourt towards the entrance to the guest house, he saw Pam Gordon hurrying out towards him.

'Where have you been?' she demanded. 'I've been looking for you!'

'Talking to Robbie MacClain,' he said. 'Trying to get him to work with us.'

'Any luck?'

Jake shook his head.

'I'm afraid not,' he said.

Pam Gordon held out a sheet of paper to him.

'Anyway, you've got your deal,' she said.

Jake snatched the paper off her and read it quickly, and then more thoroughly. It agreed that, if Jake were

137

to offer his full assistance and the book was recovered and handed to 'the appropriate services', then Lauren Graham would be allowed to return legally to the United Kingdom, and Jacob Wells could return to his former job as press officer at the Department of Science. The letter was signed by Gareth Findlay-Weston, and dated that day.

'The wonders of modern communications technology,' she said. 'So all you have to do is get the book.'

Suddenly she collapsed in front of Jake, uttering a moan of pain, thudding down on to the gravel of the forecourt. Jake was dimly aware of hearing what sounded like the echo of a shot from a distance. Then something plucked at Jake's sleeve and smashed into a nearby water barrel. He was being shot at! He turned to dive behind the water barrel, and as he did so he felt a blow on the side of his head and then . . .

Chapter 19

'Where am I?'

The voice seemed to come from a long way away. Then he realised it was his own voice.

'You're in your room at Craigmount.'

Soft Scottish tones. Jeannie MacClain.

He turned to see her as she moved into his view, and a bolt of pain tore through his head.

'Aaargh!' he groaned.

'Don't move,' said Jeannie. 'The doctor said the bullet just grazed your skull, but it took a chip of bone out. Only a small chip, but painful. You were very lucky, but you need to rest.'

He was aware of bandages around his head, like a turban. He lay there flat, looking about him as best he could without moving his head, eyes going left and right, then upwards.

He recognised the decor. It was the room at the

guest house he and Lauren shared. Or, had shared, before she disappeared.

'The doctor said he thought it best to leave you here,' said Jeannie. 'There's no hospital on the island, and he thought, as your injury isn't life-threatening, you'd be better off here than being transferred to the mainland.'

'What about Mrs Gordon?'

'She's alive, but the bullet broke her leg. The air ambulance took her to Oban. She's in hospital there. They say she'll be all right.' She looked worried. 'You're both lucky to be alive.'

'Do they know who shot us?'

Jeannie shook her head.

'Now, rest,' she said. 'The doctor's given you pain-killers and something to help you sleep. He'll be back tomorrow to check on you.'

'Lauren?' said Jake.

'Who?' asked Jeannie.

I mean Helen, he thought. Helen Cooper. I feel tired. Very tired. My head feels numb. I'll ask about Helen tomorrow . . .

He woke at some time in the early hours of the morning. It was dark. Everything was dark. There was no light at all.

I have to get up and find Lauren, he thought, and he

tried to sit up in bed, but then he felt weak, all his energy fading and slipping away from him, and he sagged back on to the bed . . .

'It looks good,' said the doctor, examining the side of Jake's head.

Dr Patel. A young doctor. He had checked Jake's pulse and heart and breathing before he'd begun unravelling the bandages from around his head. A close inspection of the wound, followed by a satisfied grunt.

'Very clean,' said the doctor. 'No infection. And, luckily for you, the bullet only grazed you. There's no permanent damage. Comparatively, it's little more than having a bang on the head. Of course, it will continue to hurt for a while, but you have a very thick skull, which is fortunate.'

'How long do I have to stay here?' asked Jake.

He was fed up with lying in this bed as if he was an invalid. Lauren was out there somewhere!

'You can get up today,' said Dr Patel. 'But don't do anything too energetic to start with. Take it easy. Sit around the lounge. Or in the garden outside. Some fresh air will do you good.'

He set to work re-dressing the wound, this time using plasters.

'I have had to shave the area around your wound, so

you may feel you look a little odd,' said the doctor. 'But you can always wear a hat.'

He finished dressing the wound, and nodded approvingly at his own handiwork.

'A very neat job, though I say it myself.' He began to pack his bag, and added, 'The police want to talk to you, of course.'

The police again, groaned Jake. He seemed to have spent most of his time on Mull being questioned by them.

'Are they here?'

Dr Patel nodded.

'They're waiting downstairs. A Detective Sergeant Stewart and a constable.' He gave Jake a wry smile. 'It might be as well to talk to them now and get it over with, then you can rest.'

'I suppose so,' agreed Jake.

'So, shall I tell them they can come up?'

'OK,' said Jake.

'Good. I shall call in on you again tomorrow. I've left some painkillers on your bedside table. If you feel the need, by all means take them. You can take two at one time, but no more than two every four hours. Is that understood?'

'Yes,' said Jake. He was tempted to nod, but knew if he did, it'd hurt his head.

'And if anything gets worse, or if you're worried,

just get Mrs MacClain to call me. I'm available twenty-four hours a day.'

He headed for the door.

'I'll tell Sergeant Stewart he can come and see you, but I'll ask him to go gently with you. And not to keep asking questions for too long.'

Jake smiled his thanks, and let himself sink back against the pillows. His head still ached, but not as badly as it had done the day before. I'm not doing badly for a guy who got shot in the head, he told himself.

There was a brisk knock at his door, then it opened and Sergeant Stewart walked in, followed by the same constable who'd arrested Jake and taken him off in handcuffs.

'The doctor says you're fit enough to answer questions,' said Stewart.

'Just a few,' Jake said.

Stewart regarded Jake suspiciously.

'I don't think I'm going to get many useful answers anyway, do you?' he demanded.

'That depends,' said Jake. 'If I can help, I will.'

'Right,' said Stewart. He pulled a chair close to the bed and sat down on it, leaving the constable standing.

'So, what's the connection between you and Mrs Pamela Gordon?' he asked.

'We're both staying at this guest house,' said Jake. 'Apart from that, there's no connection.'

143

'And yet she came and took you out of police custody after you were being questioned about the murder of her husband.'

'Yes,' said Jake.

Stewart studied Jake for a moment, then said, 'She gave me a phone number to call. It turned out to be British intelligence. They ordered me to release you into her custody. Why would that be?'

'I have no idea,' said Jake.

'It can only be because you're either also working for British intelligence, or because they have first claim on you as a suspect.'

'Or because I was innocent.'

'If that was the case, it would have been left to a lawyer to deal with it. British intelligence putting their oar in and ordering your release suggests something else.'

'What can I say?' said Jake. 'I don't know why they did that. Perhaps you'd better ask Mrs Gordon?'

'My colleagues in Oban are doing that as we speak,' said Stewart. 'But she seems as reluctant to tell us what's going on as you.' Changing tack, he asked, 'Why were you both shot?'

'I have no idea,' said Jake. 'If it crossed my mind that we were going to be targets, we'd have been more careful.'

'So you can't think of anyone who'd want to harm you or Mrs Gordon?'

144

'No,' said Jake. 'Anyway, shouldn't you be out looking for Helen, instead of talking to me? You know where I am if you need me. Helen is out there somewhere. She could be stuck down a crevice, or in a cave, or anywhere. She could be unconscious.'

'We know, and we've got that in hand,' said Stewart.

'In hand, how?' demanded Jake.

'We're liaising with search and rescue and the coast-guard,' Stewart said. 'We're going to implement a search.'

Good, thought Jake. He didn't think that Lauren was lost on the island anywhere, but if she was being held prisoner in some outbuilding, they might find her. Unless, as Jake suspected, the Russians were holding her, in which case they'd resist any attempts to search their premises, claiming diplomatic immunity. But at least a search of the island would eliminate her being trapped in some cove.

Jake looked at Stewart, who was still regarding him with that suspicious glare. I need to get him out of here so I can get on with my own search for Lauren, thought Jake. He let out a small groan.

'Actually, my head's starting to pound a bit. Would you mind if we left it there for the moment? I can always answer any questions later. After all, I'm not going anywhere.'

Stewart continued to fix Jake with his baleful glare.

After what seemed an age of an almost threatening silence, the detective sergeant grunted and said, 'We have very little crime here because people behave, and we do a good job, which suits me. But when something big like this happens and I'm told to stay away from it by British intelligence, I feel insulted. I don't take kindly to not being allowed to do my job properly.

'So I'm going to be keeping an eye on you, Mr Wells. And I'm asking Constable Frierson here to do the same. Purely for your own safety, you understand. We wouldn't want to disobey orders and put our noses where they're not wanted.' He stood up, jerked his thumb at the constable and the two of them left the room.

Chapter 20

After Stewart had gone, Jake lay in the bed and thought about his next move. He could get up, the doctor had said so. Nothing too strenuous. But he'd also said that fresh air would do Jake good. Well, there was fresh air around the Russians' cottage. He'd start there.

He was about to get out of bed when there was a knock on his door. Jake wondered if it was the police returning.

'Yes?' he said, doing his best to sound weak and fragile.

The door opened and the concerned face of Ian Muir looked in.

'Hi,' he said. 'I hope you don't mind my looking in, but I thought, think of this as a hospital visit. You know, neighbours seeing how the other one is, that kind of thing.'

'Sure,' said Jake. 'Come in and sit down.'

Muir nodded, came into the room, pushed the door shut, then hauled a chair over to Jake's bedside.

'How's the head?' he asked.

'Not bad. Considering someone shot at me,' he said.

'Yeah,' said Muir, still looking concerned. 'Pam Gordon didn't get off so lucky.'

'No,' said Jake. 'But at least she's alive.'

'True.' Muir nodded. 'So, do the cops have any idea who shot you both?'

'No idea at all,' said Jake.

'How about — why?' asked Muir. 'I mean, have they got any clue as to motive, or are we talking about some mad serial killer roaming the island?'

'Worried?' asked Jake.

'You bet your life I am!' said Muir. 'I mean, is it even safe to go walking around here?' He frowned again as he asked, 'Any word on your girlfriend? I understand she's disappeared. The word is that she's been snatched.'

'No,' sighed Jake. 'There's been no sign of her.'

'I hear there's talk of bringing people over from the mainland to mount a search for her,' said Muir. 'If that happens, count me in. I've started to get to know this area pretty good since I've been here.'

'Thanks,' said Jake. 'I guess the police will be handling that.'

'Any word from the doc?' asked Muir. 'You know, about when you can get up?'

148

'Today, he says,' Jake told him. 'The bullet just chipped the bone. Nothing serious.'

Muir grunted.

'A bullet in the head sounds serious to me,' he commented.

'Not in the head,' Jake corrected him. 'It bounced off.' He grinned. 'Luckily I must have a pretty thick skull.'

Muir sighed and shook his head sadly.

'When I booked to come here I never thought of this as a dangerous place,' he said. 'Dougie MacClain dead, John Gordon stabbed, you and Pam Gordon shot, your girlfriend Helen being snatched. My God, we don't even get that on our bad days in Chicago!' He gave Jake a serious and concerned look. 'Listen, if there's anything I can do, if you need anything . . .'

'No, I'm fine thanks,' said Jake. 'The MacClains are taking really good care of me. And, like I say, I can be back on my feet today. In fact, I thought I'd get up once you've gone and take a walk.'

Muir frowned again.

'If you want my opinion, you ought to think twice about going anywhere on this island right at this moment. Someone shot you once. Who knows, they might get luckier next time.'

'It's a chance, but I can't stay here for ever,' said Jake.

149

'OK, I'll let you get yourself ready,' said Muir. He stood up. 'The police have no idea who shot you, or why?' he enquired again.

'No idea at all,' said Jake.

'Well, let's hope it wasn't personal,' said Muir.

He headed for the door. At the door, he turned to Jake. 'Remember what I said about looking for Helen. As soon as they organise a search, count me in. In the meantime, I'll keep my eyes open when I'm walking around.'

'So you're still happy to go out?' asked Jake.

'Hell, yes!' said Muir firmly. 'I came here to enjoy this place, and no murdering lunatic on the loose is gonna stop me! Anyway, who'd want to kill me?'

With that, he left.

Who'd want to kill Muir indeed, Jake wondered.

The visit by the American puzzled him. Maybe it simply was, as Muir had said, one resident making a sympathetic visit to another who'd been injured. A kind of hospital visit. But Muir had been mostly interested in finding out what the police thought were the motives for the shooting.

Jake got out of bed and dressed. His head still ached, so he took a couple of painkillers, then went downstairs. Alec MacClain was in reception.

'Mr Wells!' he exclaimed when he saw Jake. 'You didn't need to get up! We'd have brought you up anything you wanted. All you had to do was phone down from your room.'

'I'm fine,' Jake assured him. 'Well, fine-*ish*,' he admitted. 'Anyway, Dr Patel said he thought it would be better for me to get up.' He looked around to make sure there was no one else within earshot, then asked, 'Anything happened?'

Alec MacClain sighed. 'There's been no sign of your friend, I'm afraid. The police tell me they're going to mount a major search tomorrow. They're bringing in coastguard teams, search and rescue and volunteers, and they'll be covering every square inch.'

They won't find her, realised Jake. Whoever took Lauren is keeping her under lock and key. If she's still alive, that is. Angrily, he tried to dismiss the possibility that she wasn't from his mind. She's alive! he told himself. She *must* be!

Alec MacClain leant towards Jake and muttered, 'The two Russians are back. The ones who went to the mainland. They came back on the ferry this morning.'

'Does anyone know where they've been?'

Alec shook his head.

'No, but the best guess is Glasgow or Edinburgh.'

'So, whatever they went to get, they've brought back,' said Jake thoughtfully.

'That's what it looks like,' agreed Alec.

The materials to create spontaneous human

combustion. To make a human body burst into flames. And they'd only be doing that if they wanted to test them out. And, the fact that they'd come back to Mull meant they were planning to test them here, on the island. On someone. A human specimen.

Lauren.

I have to stop them, thought Jake. He had to get into the Russians' cottage. He was sure that was where Lauren was being kept prisoner.

The two Russians were back with the necessary ingredients. The experiment would be taking place any time now.

I have to go in, thought Jake. I have to go in *now*.

Chapter 21

Jake returned to his room and put on his jacket, then slipped a small torch into his pocket. He would need it to make his way through the tunnel, away from any daylight. He looked out of the window. Not that there was much daylight left; the evening darkness was starting to descend. He hoped the darkness would give him the cover he needed.

He went carefully and quietly down the stairs. If he could, he hoped to get to the cave and the secret tunnel without anyone seeing him. He felt confident in the MacClain family, but bitter experience in the past had shown him that, as far as the Malichea books were concerned, no one was to be trusted.

He made it out of the guest house unseen, but as he set off down the cliffside path to the shore, he ran into Rona coming up.

'Mr Wells!' she said, alarmed. 'Should you be out?'

'Yes,' Jake assured her. 'But I'd rather you didn't say anything to anyone apart from your parents.'

She looked troubled.

'There's still no sign of your friend,' she said.

'No,' said Jake. 'So I understand.' He looked past her, down towards the shore. 'Where's Robbie?'

She let out a heartfelt sigh.

'I don't know,' she said. 'I've just been along to the boat shed, looking for him.' She looked appealingly at Jake. 'I'm worried that he's going to do something stupid. If you see him, will you stop him?'

'I'll do what I can,' said Jake. 'But I don't think what I say carries much weight with your brother. Anyway, I'd better be moving along.'

'You're going into the tunnel, aren't you?' she said. 'Into the Russians' cottage.'

Jake hesitated, then he nodded.

'Yes,' he said.

'Let me come with you!' Rona begged.

'No,' said Jake firmly. 'We've seen what these people can do. If you went in and anything happened to you, it would kill your parents.' And they'd kill me, thought Jake to himself.

It was the best argument he could have put to her. He saw her face fall as she thought about her parents. She nodded.

'What shall I do if you're not back?' she asked.

Jake did his best to put on a confident smile.

'Add me to the list of people the search and rescue team are looking for.' He grinned.

It was a confidence he didn't feel at all. He was going into the enemy's den, alone and unarmed, with no plan as to what he was going to do once he was inside.

He gave Rona a wink, and then set off down the steep path to the shore.

He walked along the shingled beach, stumbling slightly on the uneven ground in the gathering darkness as he moved. Finally, he came to the narrow cave that led to the secret tunnel. He checked that no one seemed to be watching, and then he slipped into the cave.

The barnacle-encrusted wooden boards that hid the entrance seemed to be in the same place where he, Lauren and Rona had left them on their last visit. He hoped that meant that Robbie hadn't come this way. But then Robbie had told Jake very firmly that he had no intention of using the tunnel. But that didn't mean Robbie wouldn't.

Jake switched on the torch and heaved the heavy boards aside. The effort it took made his head start to ache again. What was it the doctor had told him? Nothing strenuous. Yes, well, all that was out of the window. There was only one thing that mattered now, and that was getting Lauren back safely.

He found the steep steps carved into the rocks and began to climb them. At times they were so narrow he had to use his hands and knees, but finally he could hear voices above him, and knew he was getting to the top.

He switched off the torch and allowed his eyes to get used to the darkness. Then he climbed slowly up the last few steps. All the time the voices, though muffled, were getting louder. Finally he came to a wooden partition. This must be the back of the cupboard, he thought. There was a small hole in the wood, and Jake peered carefully through and saw an empty cupboard in front of him. Empty, that is, except for some dust-covered bottles on a shelf.

Good, he thought. No one should want to open this cupboard to get anything.

Jake looked for a latch or some kind of catch in the wooden partition; and found it at one side. As quietly as he could, he pulled on the catch, and the wooden partition opened like a door.

Jake crept in. He worked his way towards the actual door of the cupboard, which was just an arm's length away. There was another hole in this piece of wood. He put his eye to the hole, and had to dig his fingernails into his palms to stop himself yelling out.

Lauren was there, tied to a chair. At the far back of the room, near to the door, were two tough-looking

Russians, both with pistols in holsters strapped to their belts.

Jake twisted to try to get a better view of the room, and saw the tall figure of Professor Lemski come into focus. The professor was standing next to Lauren, drumming his fingers on a small wooden table next to her. On the small table Jake saw the familiar black-leather casing, embossed with the symbol of the Order of Malichea, which he recognised as the protective cover for the book. The book itself lay open on the table. Next to it were some racks of test tubes filled with different sorts of liquid, and in front of them was a hypodermic needle, with a yellowish liquid inside.

'As I was saying, you're presence here is very oppor-tune, Ms Graham,' said Lemski.

Jake saw Lauren glare at Lemski.

'And as I've already told you, my name is Helen Cooper,' she said. 'I am from New Zealand . . .'

'Please, spare us the cover story,' said Lemski with a sigh. 'We knew who you were soon after you arrived. Your fame precedes you.'

Lauren looked puzzled.

'What do you mean "fame"?' she asked.

'We are both interested in the same areas of science,' said Lemski. 'It is natural that someone like myself should check on what others in the same field are doing. I discovered your account of the history of the

157

Order of Malichea, and the hidden library, some time ago, and followed your researches devoutly until they were terminated by British intelligence.'

Lauren still looked puzzled.

'I didn't publish anything,' she said. 'Not in print or on the net.'

'You didn't need to,' said Lemski. 'Once you had checked out a website about Malichea that we had set up, we had access to your computer. Our technical people are very advanced in their use of surveillance techniques. Better than your own MI5.'

'So you hacked into my computer and you've been spying on me?'

Lemski nodded.

'And not just during your time in England. Once we learnt that you had been exiled to New Zealand . . .'

'How did you discover that?' asked Lauren.

Lemski smiled.

'Please. Every security service has agents inside those of other countries. You British have yours in ours; we have our people inside yours. It is the same whether it's the Americans, the Chinese, the French . . . whoever.' He smiled. 'There are very few secrets in the world of secrets.'

'Can we get on with it?' growled another voice. An American. It was Muir!

The American came into view, a scowl on his face as

he said, 'Let's see if this thing works! That's what we're here to do! Time is money!'

Lemski turned to the American and shook his head disapprovingly.

'Patience, please, Mr Muir,' he murmured. He tapped the open book. 'This information has lain hidden for hundreds of years. It should be savoured, not rushed. Remember, that until Ms Graham arrived on the scene in this timely fashion, we might have had to wait until I returned to Russia before testing it out.'

'Don't give me that!' snapped Muir. 'We were always going to find someone local to test it out on.'

Lauren looked apprehensively at the book, and at the hypodermic syringe.

'Test it out?' she asked, and Jake could detect the note of fear in her voice.

'Of course.' Lemski nodded. 'You know what this book is about, of course?'

Lauren shook her head. Lemski sighed.

'Really, Ms Graham, I wonder why you bother with this pretence. It won't help your situation. It concerns spontaneous human combustion. More precisely, the book contains the formula for an elixir to create it.' He looked thoughtful. 'It is based on observations Dioscorides made of the conditions under which it occurs in humans. We have tried to create the condition ourselves, but unfortunately — although they have succeeded — our formulae have had their limitations. In particular, they take too long to take effect.'

'Just like you're taking too long to get on with it!' growled Muir. 'What is it with you Ruskies! All this talk!'

Yes, please keep talking, Jake begged silently. With a sick feeling, he now knew what they were going to do. They were going to inject Lauren with the formula in the hypodermic, and hope to set off a reaction in which she would burst into flames. I have to stop them! thought Jake. But how?

As well as Lemski and Muir, there were the two other Russians in the room, both armed. They'd shoot him dead as soon as he burst out from his hiding place. His only hope was that Lemski would keep on talking long enough for Jake to come up with something. Some diversion. But even if he did, how would Lauren be able to get away? She was bound securely to the chair.

Suddenly there was shouting outside the door, an angry voice yelling and other raised voices talking in Russian. Then the door burst open and two Russians came in, dragging Robbie between them. Robbie's hands had been cable-tied together behind his back, and there was a livid bruise over one eye, and blood around his nose and mouth.

One of the Russians said something to the professor, who nodded, and replied in Russian. At once, the two

160

other Russians in the room pulled a chair over, sat Robbie in it and began to tie him up, ropes going around his legs and wrists, the same as Lauren's bonds.

'Well, well,' said Lemski. 'This is getting exciting, don't you think, Mr Muir?'

'You won't get away with this!' raged Robbie.

'Oh, I think we will,' said Lemski confidently. 'After all, we got away with getting rid of your uncle when we caught him nosing around.' He looked pointedly at Muir. 'Although it was a very unsubtle way to dispose of him. Personally, I'd have preferred to have kept him for something like this.'

'I didn't have much choice,' said Muir. 'He came at me. I had to defend myself. And anyway, at that stage you didn't have the book, and we weren't sure you were going to find it.'

'I was always sure we were going to find it,' countered Lemski flatly. 'The fact that Mr MacClain defended it so fiercely told me it was definitely hidden at this site.'

'I'll kill you for what you did to my uncle!' Robbie spat furiously.

'I doubt that,' said Lemski calmly. He smiled. 'In fact your arrival gives me a choice. Which one of you to use first for the experiment.'

Robbie looked at Lemski warily.

'What experiment?' he demanded.

161

'He's going to inject us with some stuff he's made,' said Lauren. 'The formula was in the book. If it works, we'll burst into flames.'

Robbie looked shocked.

'That was what the book was about?'

Lauren nodded.

'Yes,' she said. 'And now it's out in the open.'

Robbie shook his head.

'That's not possible,' he said. 'There's no such thing. It won't work.'

'Oh yes there is,' said Lemski. 'We've been conducting experiments along this line for some time in Russia. Our big problem has been the time it takes for the reaction to happen. Too long. It allows time for our enemies to take some kind of action against us before combustion happens.' He tapped the open book. 'We're about to find out if Disciorides has the answer to that problem.'

'So can we finally do it?' demanded Muir impatiently.

'Yes.' Lemski nodded. He looked at Robbie, and at Lauren. 'The question now is, which one of you goes first.'

'Do them both,' said Muir.

'No,' said Lemski. 'We need to keep one in reserve to double-check the results.' He said something in Russian, and two of the Russians left the room. Muir frowned.

162

'What's happening?' he said. 'Why have you sent them to set up the byre? What's wrong with doing it here?'

Professor Lemski looked at him with the air of someone lecturing a not very bright pupil.

'This room has wooden panelling, wooden floors, and wooden supports for the ceiling. Do you really think it a good idea to start a fire in here?'

'But spontaneous human combustion is supposed to happen without damaging the area immediately around,' said Muir.

'And you think it worth taking that chance?' asked Lemski sarcastically. 'The byre is made of stone. Perfectly safe.' He said something in Russian to the two remaining men, and then gestured to Muir. 'Come, let us make sure that everything is ready for the experiment. And while we do that, we can discuss which of these two will be our first guinea pig.'

Muir hesitated. He was obviously keen to get going, inject either Lauren or Robbie at once, but then he shrugged and left the room. Just before Lemski followed him, Lemski gave a last order in Russian; then the professor went out, pulling the door shut after him.

As Jake watched, the taller of the two men went to a cupboard and produced a roll of tape. Jake guessed they were going to gag Lauren and Robbie to stop them shouting out. Not that there was much chance of anyone hearing them at this remote spot; but they would have to drag them across open ground to the byre outside, and there was more chance of a shout for help being heard.

The tall man with the tape went to Lauren first and tried to tape over her mouth, but Lauren kept moving her head left and right, dodging. The tall man swore and tried to hold her head still with one hand and put the tape on with the other, but Lauren continued jerking her head around so it became an impossible task for the man. The tall man snapped something in Russian, and the other man, the shorter of the two, went to Lauren and grasped her head in both hands to hold it secure.

This is my only chance! thought Jake. It's now or never! He picked up one of the dusty bottles, kicked open the cupboard door, and hurled himself into the room, swinging the bottle down hard on the head of the tall man. The bottle smashed and the tall man collapsed. The shorter man gaped at Jake, shocked by his sudden appearance. And then he reached for the gun in his holster.

Desperately, Jake snatched up the nearest object, the hypodermic needle lying on the table, and hurled it at the man with all his might. The long needle went through the man's shirt into his chest. The man stumbled and fell backwards, and in an effort to regain his

164

balance reached out towards Robbie, but he fell and banged the plunger of the hypodermic against the bound boy's arm.

The man looked down at the hypodermic sticking out of him, the plunger now pressed in. He fell back, pulling at the hypodermic, tearing it out of his body, but even as he did so smoke began to rise from his skin. He screamed, a shrilly dreadful noise, and then his scream was cut off as smoke poured out of his mouth and nostrils . . . and then there was a blinding white flash, and his body was enveloped in flames.

Jake was only aware of this out of the corner of his eye, he was already using the sharp glass from the broken bottle to cut through the ropes that tied Lauren to the chair. As she came free, he turned his attention to Robbie.

Lauren stumbled to her feet, and Jake saw that her eyes were fixed in horror on the burning man, covered in flames from his ankles to the top of his head.

'Help me!' Jake urged her. Lauren snapped out of her trance, snatching up another piece of broken glass and set to work cutting the ropes around Robbie's ankles as Jake freed the boy's wrists. Outside, they could hear running footsteps approaching.

'The table!' yelled Jake.

Together, the three of them dragged the table across the room and placed it in front of the door. They were just in time; the door bulged inwards as weight was thrown against it. From outside came angry shouts in Russian, and then Muir's voice calling, 'What the hell's going on?'

Jake gave the table one last push into place as Lauren snatched up the book, and followed Robbie, running for the cupboard, and the secret back entrance to the tunnel. Not that it was a secret any longer; the cupboard door was hanging open and shattered from Jake's kick. And there was no time to slip the back of the cupboard into place; the enemy would be inside this room any moment. As Jake turned to follow Lauren and Robbie, there was the deafening sound of gunfire. Splinters of wood tore into the room from the door and Jake felt something rip at his jacket. A bullet! Jake hurled himself forward across the room, into the cupboard, as more bullets were fired blindly from the other side of the door.

As Jake dived into the tunnel, he heard a crash as the table was smashed back. They were in the room! By then he was running, almost falling down the stone steps of the tunnel, aware that their enemies were now very close behind them, armed, and ready to kill.

Chapter 22

Jake half ran, half fell down the stone steps of the tunnel, running blind and crashing into the rock walls.

He pulled the torch from his pocket and shone it on the steps, and hurried down, following the beam as it twisted and turned, stumbling in his urgency to get away. Behind him he could hear shouts in Russian, orders being given, and then heavy footsteps on rock.

Jake pushed himself to go faster, and as he did so he felt something grab him by the jacket and drag him to one side.

'Turn off the torch!' rasped a voice in his ear. Robbie.

Jake switched it off, and felt himself being dragged further into what seemed to be some kind of dead-end niche off the steeply stepped tunnel.

Lights blazed as the beams of torches lit up the tunnel, casting flickering shadows at the edge of their hiding place. Then the sound of boots crashing on the stone steps raced past them, heading down. As the lights disappeared, Jake found himself standing in pitch-blackness.

Robbie waited for a few minutes, then he whispered, 'Give me your torch.'

Jake handed him the torch, and Robbie switched it on and shone it into the narrow niche where they were standing. Jake saw Lauren further along, and — beyond her — a very, very narrow crevice. Robbie shone his torch into this crevice, and Jake realised it was a tunnel, even narrower than the tunnel he'd gone through to get to the cupboard.

'We go this way,' whispered Robbie. 'Stay close behind me, and watch your footing. It's a bit narrow in places, but we should all make it through.'

Jake and Lauren followed Robbie, staying close to him as instructed, as they squeezed and pushed their way between slimy wet rock faces.

'This comes out on the other side of the headland,' said Robbie. 'Rona and I used to play in it when we were small.'

'Didn't your parents ever get worried about you, doing this?' asked Lauren. 'You could have got lost or trapped.'

'We never told them,' said Robbie.

They moved on, down, down, down, the rocks slippery underfoot. At times the passage became so narrow that Jake was worried he wouldn't be able to make it through the small openings.

'How much longer?' he whispered.

'Nearly there,' replied Robbie.

Suddenly Jake became aware that the gaps seemed to be widening.

'I'm going to turn off the torch,' whispered Robbie. 'We're coming to the point where the cave goes out to the shore. That light will give us away.'

He switched the torch off, and they were plunged into blackness.

'I can't see,' complained Jake.

'Give it a minute or two to allow your eyes to adjust,' said Robbie.

The three of them stood there, in the darkness, and slowly Jake saw what Robbie meant: a trickle of very faint light was coming along the tunnel.

'OK,' said Robbie. 'Move slowly. Watch where you walk. And keep quiet.'

Robbie led the way, Lauren and Jake following, as they crept slowly along the last few metres of narrow rock tunnel. Now the ambient light of night from outside guided them as they saw the opening of the cave, and the sea ahead of them.

They reached the edge of the cave and stood, listening. Above them on the cliff top they could hear shouting, and they saw the night sky being lit up.

'They're using torches,' whispered Robbie.

Even as he spoke, a beam of light from a powerful torch above them hit the shingle beach right in front of the cave opening. It lingered there, then moved on.

'We can't get back to the house this way,' whispered Robbie. 'They'll spot us for sure.'

'What about the other cave?' asked Jake. 'The one they thought they were following us down?'

'That comes out on the other side of the headland,' said Robbie.

'So they'll come round the headland and come to this cave?' asked Lauren.

Robbie nodded.

'They could also come back through that tunnel and find the way we came, down that side-tunnel,' murmured Jake.

'Whatever they do, if we stay here, they'll find us,' said Robbie.

'And if we try to make it along the shore, their torches will pick us out,' said Jake.

'We're trapped,' whispered Lauren.

'You forget, this is the twenty-first century,' said Jake. 'Mobile phones.'

'They took mine off me,' said Lauren.

'And mine,' said Robbie.

'But they didn't take mine,' said Jake.

He reached into his pocket and pulled out his mobile

phone, and then his face fell. The bullet that had hit his jacket had smashed his phone beyond repair.

Outside, they could hear more urgent shouting in Russian.

'OK,' admitted Jake unhappily. 'We're trapped.'

'Maybe there's a chance,' murmured Robbie.

'What is it?' asked Jake.

'There's a rowing boat just along the shore. Just a small one. It's Dougie's, but he hardly ever used it.' In the half-light Jake saw a wistful smile cross Robbie's face. 'He preferred boats with engines.'

'You're suggesting we row to somewhere further along the shore?' asked Jake.

'No.' Robbie shook his head. 'They'll be watching for us all the way along the shore. I'm thinking we row out to Patrick's Island.'

'Where's that?' asked Lauren.

'It's a very small island about a mile offshore. If we make it, we can hide out there until we see the search parties come out tomorrow, and get their attention.'

'What search parties?' queried Lauren.

'Police, coastguard, search and rescue, and other volunteers,' explained Jake. 'Looking for you.'

'Dad said they'll be starting out tomorrow morning,' Robbie added.

'What are the chances of us reaching this boat alive and getting away?' asked Lauren.

'It's the only one we've got,' said Robbie. 'If we stay here, we'll be killed. If we try and make it along the shore, we'll be killed.'

'The boat it is.' Jake nodded.

'Stay close to the cliffs,' Robbie ordered them. 'There's a bit of an overhang that should hide us from their torches until we get to the boat.'

'And once we get to the boat?' asked Lauren.

Robbie gave a doubtful sigh.

'Then, it's up to good luck,' he said.

They crept along the shingle, hugging close to the cliff, all too aware of the voices above them calling to one another in Russian, and the torch beams shining down on the shore just a metre away from them. They hardly dared breathe in case it might be heard by the people hunting them.

Finally, they came to the rowing boat tied to a wooden post hammered into the beach. Even here, the beams of torches were still searching for them, light coming down from above and scanning the shore just a few metres away. They stood, hiding, until after what seemed an age the torchlights moved away inland. Immediately, Robbie darted out and set to work unfastening the mooring rope. When it was free, he gestured to Jake and Lauren to stand ready to help push the small boat across the shingle to the water.

'Wait until they've moved away,' he whispered, gesturing upwards towards the cliff top.

'Say they don't?' asked Jake.

'They will,' said Robbie. 'When you're doing a search, you don't just stay in one place. They've been on the cliff path for a good while now. They're bound to move further inland in a minute or two.'

'If they do, maybe we could still make it along the water's edge in the boat?' suggested Lauren. 'Land somewhere nearer the path to your place?'

'Not a good idea,' whispered back Robbie. 'They'll definitely have people watching all the paths to our place. That's where they'll expect us to go. And if we stay too close to the shore, there's a chance they'll hear the oars.'

'So Patrick's Island sounds the safest place for us at this moment,' said Jake.

'If we can get there,' added Lauren fearfully.

The three stood in the darkness of the cliff, tense, hands on the edge of the small boat, listening. After an agonising wait, as Robbie had predicted, they heard the voices of the Russians move away from the cliff path directly above them as the search headed inland.

'Now!' whispered Robbie urgently.

They pushed at the boat, the feeling of fear inside each giving them extra strength, and the rowing boat slid over the shingle. Almost immediately they were up to their calves in the cold water.

'Get in!'

Jake and Lauren clambered aboard the boat, and Robbie continued pushing it further out into the water until he was up to his waist, before he climbed aboard with them.

He slotted the two oars into the rowlocks, and began heading out, using long strokes. Jake was impressed by the way the blades of the oars cut through the water, pushing the boat along, but without any splashing noises. Jake knew that if *he'd* tried rowing, there would have been a lot of splashing going on, and the beams from the torches would have soon been shining on them, followed by a hail of bullets.

Robbie continued rowing, pulling hard at the oars. Jake looked back towards the shore, and now he could see on the cliff top the criss-crossing of beams of light, and even from this distance they could hear voices raised. As he watched, he saw the beams of light from torches appear from around the headland and move along the shore towards the very narrow cave they'd come out of just a brief while before. Other beams of light were moving along the shore from the other direction, from the direction of the guest house.

We'd have been caught if we'd stayed on shore, reflected Jake. Well done, Robbie.

They were lucky that there were clouds in the sky, obscuring the moon, otherwise they'd have made a sitting target. As it was, Jake felt nervous the whole time they were out on the water, exposed. All the time he was waiting for a torch beam to turn their way and pick them out, and guns to begin firing.

Jake kept his eyes fixed on the Russians on the cliffs. The lights from their torches were specks now, small from this distance.

'We're coming in to land,' whispered Lauren beside him.

Jake turned his head and saw the heavily wooded tiny island fast approaching. Robbie stopped rowing strongly, and let the small boat drift in. As they felt the sand and shingle beneath them pull the boat to a halt, Robbie dropped the oars and leapt out into the water.

'Come on,' he said. 'We've got to get it out of sight.'

Jake and Lauren dropped overboard and joined Robbie in the water, which was past their knees. The coldness of it took Jake's breath away.

The three of them worked together to drag the small boat up on to the shore, and then continued dragging it over shingle into the thick wood that came right down to the beach.

Robbie disappeared into the wood, and reappeared dragging branches, which he proceeded to put over the boat, concealing it further.

'We'll stay near the shore until just before dawn comes,' he told the other two. 'If you try and scramble through this wood in the dark, there's a chance you'll put your foot in a hole and twist your ankle.'

They settled down in the cover of the trees.

'I'm freezing,' said Jake, indicating his soaking-wet trousers.

'You'll be even colder if you take them off,' advised Robbie. 'The best thing you can do is keep them on and let them dry on you once the sun starts to come up.'

'I wonder when the police will be starting the search?' asked Jake.

'My guess is mid-morning,' said Robbie. 'Remember, they have to wait for the tides to bring the boats over from the mainland.'

'So all we have to do is stay hidden until the search starts.' Lauren nodded.

'And hope we can get their attention so they get to us before the Russians do,' added Jake.

Chapter 23

They took turns to keep watch, one awake and watching the far shore while the other two slept. At least, that was the theory, but Jake couldn't sleep. Too much had happened, and now the Russians were just a short distance away, searching for them. The Russians would be after the book. For a fleeting moment Jake thought about giving it back to them, that might save their lives. Then he dismissed the idea. The Russians — or Muir — had already killed to protect the search for the book. Jake was sure there would be no mercy shown to them if Muir and the Russians caught them. They'd be as good as dead, whether they handed over the book or not.

He stayed awake for the rest of the night, closing his eyes now and then and hoping to rest, but every tiny noise made his eyes open and his body jerk up and shoot a look towards the shore. It was a relief when the first streaks of light began to break up the night sky as dawn arrived.

Lauren was on watch, and Jake saw her straining her eyes over the water, to where the search was still continuing.

'What's happening?' he asked.

'Nothing,' said Lauren.

'We need to go inland now,' said Robbie's voice behind them. 'Up to higher ground.'

Jake turned to him.

'Did you get any sleep?' he asked.

Robbie shook his head.

'No,' he said. 'You two?'

Both Jake and Lauren shook their heads.

'Too much adrenalin pumping,' said Lauren.

'Well, let's hope tiredness doesn't slow us down,' said Robbie. 'Now it's daylight, we're going to need to be on our guard more than ever.'

He made his way into the dense woodland that fringed the tiny island, and Jake and Lauren followed him as he pushed his way between trees and bushes.

The ground rose sharply, and they found themselves climbing. Robbie stopped when they came to a scattering of stones in a clearing. Some of the stones were lying about on the ground, others were heaped in piles.

'What's this?' asked Jake.

'Patrick's house,' said Robbie. 'The island is called

Patrick's Island after a hermit who lived here hundreds and hundreds of years ago. Some reckon it was Saint Patrick himself, but I don't think so. Anyway, the stones are all that's left of his house.' He pointed upwards. 'From up there we'll be able to get a good view of Mull, and we might be able to signal from here once we see the search parties.'

They climbed higher, on open ground now, and as they rose above the trees they saw that Robbie was right, they could see right across the water to the island of Mull, and the shore they'd left from under cover of darkness. There was action going on at that same spot, people milling around, and what looked like a red boat.

'What's happening?' asked Lauren.

'It's a RIB,' said Robbie. 'Rigid inflatable. The coast-guard use them.'

'So the search has started already!' said Jake brightly. 'Excellent!'

'No,' Robbie corrected him. 'Those are the Russians. It means they've worked out where we went. They're on their way here.'

'How did they work that out?' asked Lauren.

'They must have found the marks our boat made when we pushed it to the sea, and realised that this is the only place we could have made it to.'

'What are we going to do?' asked Lauren, her voice showing her alarm. 'Get back to our boat?'

'Waste of time,' said Robbie, shaking his head. 'They'll overtake us easily, and out on the water in that boat we'd be sitting ducks.'

'And there's no sign of the search parties!' said Lauren desperately.

'I've got an idea,' said Jake. 'I hang my jacket somewhere up here, so they can see it fluttering through the trees. That'll bring them up here. Meanwhile, we get back down near the shore and hide there. When they come up here, we grab their boat.'

'That's crazy!' protested Lauren. 'They're bound to leave someone guarding the boat, and they'll be armed!'

'You got a better idea?' asked Jake.

They looked towards the far shore. People were getting into the inflatable. Even from this distance, they could make out the tall figure of Professor Lemski and the short squatness of Dmitri. Dmitri was getting into the boat with three other people. They all looked as if they were carrying rifles.

'OK,' said Jake. 'Here they come. Time to get down to the shore and find a place to hide.'

He slipped off his jacket and draped it from the branch of a tree at the edge of the clearing. Then he, Lauren and Robbie hurried back the way they had come, downhill towards the wooded shore.

Chapter 24

Jake, Lauren and Robbie crouched down behind the cover of the trees and bushes, their eyes on the approaching boat. Jake could see the stocky figure of Dmitri standing up, binoculars to his eyes, scanning the island. Then Jake saw him raise his arm and point and give a shout to the three other men in the boat.

'He's seen my coat,' whispered Jake.

They crouched down even lower, hardly daring to breathe, as the boat came in to land, crashing into the shingle of the beach. The four men leapt out, all of them armed with automatic rifles. Dmitri shouted orders in Russian, and then he and two of the others began to head up towards the top of the island.

'Looks like they've fallen for it,' whispered Jake.

'But how do we deal with him?' asked Lauren anxiously.

Jake looked at the man left to guard the boat. Jake

saw what Lauren meant. He was tall, powerful-looking, and he seemed very comfortable in the way he held his automatic rifle. He was also very alert, his head moving this way and that as he scanned the shore and the foliage for any sign of movement.

'It's about thirty metres to the boat,' groaned Jake. 'Too far away for us to take a run at him. He'll shoot us down before we reach him.'

'It's either that, or wait for Dmitri and his pals to come back down and find us,' said Lauren sombrely.

'There may be another way,' said Robbie. He bent down and picked up a stone. 'When we were kids, me and Rona used to play targets. We'd throw stones at things and see who could hit the most.'

'Who won?' asked Jake.

'Usually Rona,' admitted Robbie ruefully. 'She'd hit the targets nine times out of ten. But I was pretty good too. I'd hit them six times out of ten.'

'Six?' said Jake, worried. 'That's not very good odds.'

'As Rona's not here, those are the only odds we've got,' said Robbie. He weighed the stone in his hand, testing it. 'And his head's bigger than most of the things we threw stones at.'

'Yes, but your targets didn't keep moving the way he is,' pointed out Jake, as the man began to prowl on the shore in front of the boat. 'And I bet you didn't have to throw them while in hiding.'

'Stop being so negative, Jake!' hissed Lauren. 'Like Robbie says, it's our only chance.'

'That's what worries me,' said Jake.

From high up on the island, they heard shouting in Russian.

'Dmitri must have spotted it was just a jacket,' said Jake.

'In which case, now's the time,' said Robbie.

Suddenly he stepped out of their hiding place. The armed man on the shore must have heard the rustle of leaves, because he swung round towards their position, the rifle coming to bear on them, just as Robbie threw the stone.

Smack!

The stone hit the man full on the forehead. He stumbled backwards, and then collapsed, dropping the rifle.

Even before he fell, Jake, Robbie and Lauren were running towards the inflatable. As Robbie jumped into the boat, Jake stopped and scooped up the man's rifle. He checked the man. He was breathing, but out cold.

Jake threw the rifle into the boat, then he and Lauren pushed the boat off the shore and into deeper water. Robbie started the engine and Jake and Lauren threw themselves aboard.

Angry shouts from the top of the island told them they'd been spotted. Robbie opened the throttle and the boat raced away, heading out into the water and along the channel towards the path that led up to the guest house, away from the Russians' cottage. Behind them they heard gunfire from Patrick's Island. Immediately, Robbie began to zigzag the boat as bullets hit the water around them.

Robbie opened the throttle even wider and the boat sped along, leaping out of the water at points and then aquaplaning. Suddenly Robbie gave a cry of pain and fell forward, face first into the body of the boat, and the engine slowed.

'He's been shot!' yelled Lauren.

Lauren moved to Robbie and Jake saw blood high on his back, around the shoulder.

'He's conscious,' Lauren called to Jake, 'but only just.'

More shots came from the small island behind them and Jake turned. The three Russians had scrambled down to the shore and found the rowing boat. Two of them were hauling it out from its hiding place, while the third — Dmitri, by the look of it — was taking aim with his rifle at them and the boat. There was the sound of a shot; and Jake dived down, taking Lauren with him, as the bullet went over their heads, narrowly missing them.

Jake scrambled back up, taking Robbie's place at the engine, and opened up the throttle again, aiming the boat at the coast, which was now about a hundred metres away.

Another bullet zoomed past; and then there was a tearing sound, followed by a hiss of escaping air.

'They've hit the boat!' yelled Jake.

Lauren had torn Robbie's shirt open to see how bad his wound was.

'We have to get to the shore!' she shouted at Jake. 'If we don't, he'll drown. He's unconscious.'

Jake pulled back on the throttle and the boat surged forward, even though Jake could see its rubber skirt was already deflating. Sixty metres, fifty, forty . . .

The boat began to slow and sink. Twenty metres to go, ten . . .

'Out!' yelled Jake.

As the water started to come in over the deflating rubber, Jake left the throttle and grabbed Robbie under one of his arms. The sinking boat began to tip over. Lauren grabbed Robbie's other arm, and then the two of them half fell out of the capsizing boat into the cold water. Jake was relieved to find the shingle of the beach beneath his feet. Together, he and Lauren struggled to the shore, carrying Robbie's unconscious body between them. Jake looked up at the cliff top above them, but there was no sign of anyone.

'They may be lying in wait for us,' said Lauren, seeing Jake looking up at the cliff.

'We have to try, anyway,' said Jake. 'He'll die if we don't.'

They ran to the path, crouching low in case more shots came from the island; but, glancing over his shoulder, Jake saw that the three Russians were more intent on launching the rowing boat.

Robbie's body, unconscious and soaking wet, was heavy, but they managed to struggle up the steep path from the shore. The whole time, Jake expected someone to leap out of the bushes and aim a rifle at them; but they made it to the top of the path. The guest house was ahead of them.

'Not far now!' grunted Jake, and he shouldered Robbie's body higher and he and Lauren began to run.

That was when the sound of a shot rang out and the ground in front of them erupted as gunfire smashed around them.

Chapter 25

Jake and Lauren threw themselves to the ground, taking the unconscious Robbie with them.

'Don't come any nearer!'

Jake and Lauren looked at one another, startled. It was Jeannie MacClain's voice.

'Mrs MacClain!' shouted Lauren. 'We've got Robbie!'

They heard her shout out, 'Robbie!' And as they got to their feet they saw Jeannie MacClain rise up from behind the low stone wall bordering the guest house. She ran towards them, still holding the shotgun she'd fired. When she reached them, she dropped the shotgun and threw herself on her knees beside Robbie.

'He's alive,' said Lauren. 'But he needs a doctor.'

'He's been shot,' said Jake. 'We need to phone Dr Patel.'

'I can't,' said Jeannie. 'None of the phones are working.'

187

'None?' queried Lauren.

'None. And they've taken Rona and Alec!'

Jake and Lauren stared at her, shocked. She was obviously doing her best to keep control of her emotions, but the fear of everything that was happening showed clearly on her face.

'Let's get Robbie to Dr Patel,' said Jake.

'Don't move him! I'll bring the Land Rover over!' said Jeannie, and she broke into a run. Jake picked up the shotgun she'd dropped and turned around to check the path up from the shore.

'I bet it's not loaded,' said Lauren. 'She fired it at us, remember.'

'The Russians won't know that,' replied Jake.

'The Russians coming up that path will be armed,' Lauren pointed out.

Before Jake could come up with an answer, Jeannie returned over the bumpy ground at the wheel of the Land Rover. Gently, they loaded Robbie's unconscious body into the back, then Lauren climbed in beside him, while Jake joined Jeannie in the cab. As she drove, Jeannie filled them in on what had happened.

'It was less than an hour ago,' she said. 'The Russians came to the guest house. Professor Lemski with four others, all heavily armed. They took Alec and Rona with them. It happened just after the phones went down. I drove to the police station and

188

told Constable Frierson what had happened, then I came back here. I loaded up the shotgun. I'd decided I was going to go to the cottage where the Russians are and demand they hand Alec and the bairns over. They had my whole family! I wasn't going to let them do that to us!'

With one of her fists she thumped the steering wheel hard, expressing her anger.

'When I saw you coming up at the top of the path, at first I thought it was the Russians coming back; this time to take me! So I slipped out and hid behind the wall.'

'Luckily you only fired a warning shot,' said Jake.

'Professor Lemski left a message for you.'

'For me?' asked Jake.

'For you and Helen Cooper. Although he called her Ms Graham.'

Jake sighed.

'I'll explain later,' he said. 'What was the message?'

'He said you were to take the book to them at the cottage, or Alec and Rona will die. By fire, he said.'

Spontaneous human combustion, thought Jake. He'll inject them and they'll burst into flames.

'Did he give a deadline for us delivering the book to him?' asked Jake.

'Eleven o'clock this morning,' said Jeannie.

Jake looked at his watch. It was 9.30 a.m.

'An hour and a half!' he said.

Dmitri must have radioed Lemski and told him that Jake and Lauren had managed to escape from the island. Immediately, Lemski had hurried to the guest house and taken Alec and Rona hostage. That was why there had been no further chasing from Dmitri or from any of the other Russians.

'Lemski said he wants both of you to deliver the book personally,' added Jeannie. Suddenly the vehicle slowed. 'Here we are,' said Jeannie.

As they pulled up outside Dr Patel's house, Jake saw a police car parked there. Good, he thought. That saves us having to go and find them.

Jake leapt out of the Land Rover and was about to run to the doctor's house, when the door opened and Dr Patel hurried out, accompanied by Detective Sergeant Stewart and Constable Frierson.

'What's happened?' demanded Stewart. 'How did you get away?'

'Later!' said Jake. 'Robbie's in the back, and he's been shot.'

Carefully, they took Robbie from the back of the Land Rover and carried him into the doctor's house, and to the consulting room. They laid him on the medical couch.

Dr Patel examined the unconscious Robbie, then turned to them, his expression grim.

'He needs to be treated in an A&E unit,' he said. 'The best I can do is stabilise him until we can get him to the mainland.' He looked at Jeannie MacClain. 'Will you act as my nurse, Mrs MacClain? I'm afraid Donna isn't with me today, with all that's going on.'

'Of course,' said Jeannie.

'We'll leave you to it,' said Stewart. He looked point-edly at Jake and Lauren. 'We need to talk,' he said.

Jake and Lauren followed Stewart and Constable Frierson out of the house.

As they stood in front of the house, Jake reflected on how bizarre their situation was. Everything seemed so peaceful, so tranquil. The sounds of seagulls as they wheeled overhead, the quietness of the island, the vast expanse of blue sky above them, the varying shades of green of the heathlands stretching out from this small rural hamlet; and yet there was more man-made malevolent evil and danger here right at this moment than in some of the most dangerous inner cities.

'Jeannie MacClain says there are no phones work-ing,' said Jake.

'No, nor computer links. No internet, no email, either,' growled Stewart. 'I came here because Dr Patel has got a satellite phone and I thought that might work, but even that seems to be down.'

'An EMP,' said Lauren.

Stewart looked at her quizzically.

'An electromagnetic pulse,' explained Lauren. 'It disrupts electronic communications systems.'

'The Russians?' queried Stewart bitterly.

'That's my guess.' Lauren nodded. 'What's happened? Mrs MacClain told us they'd taken Alec and Rona.'

'About an hour ago,' said Stewart. 'Almost immediately after this pulse thing hit and everything went down. Professor Lemski and some of his henchmen turned up at the guest house, armed with guns, and took Rona and Alec.'

'Jeannie said he wants us to deliver the book to him,' Jake told Lauren. 'He's given a deadline of eleven o'clock. Jeannie told me about it on the way here.' He looked at his watch again. 'The clock's ticking. It's a quarter to ten. We've got seventy-five minutes.' He turned to Lauren and added: 'He said if we don't deliver it, they'll die by fire.'

'Human combustion,' said Lauren, her face going pale.

'Exactly,' said Jake.

'What do you mean "human combustion"?' demanded Stewart.

Quickly, Jake and Lauren explained to Stewart what had happened the night before: how Jake had got into the Russians' cottage and escaped with Lauren and Robbie, and how the Russian had burst into flames

192

when the hypodermic injected the toxic mixture into him.

'So this stuff is real?' said Stewart.

'Yes,' said Lauren. 'And Lemski will use it.'

'Is there anyone else on this island who can give us some kind of back-up?' asked Jake.

'There's the main station at Tobermory, in the north of the island,' said Stewart. 'But there's only one officer there, and we can't get hold of him by phone. If we drive to Tobermory, we won't get back before this deadline of the professor's. Which is why the first thing I did after Jeannie came to me this morning, was send a message by boat across to the mainland. But there's no way of knowing how far this electromagnetic pulse will have an impact. For all we know, it could have knocked out communications in Oban.'

'That depends on how big the disrupter is that's generating it,' said Lauren.

'I've asked for trained marksmen, hostage negotiators, and for help from the Russian embassy,' said Stewart. He looked at his watch. 'But, again, I doubt if they'll be able to get here before the deadline.'

'They won't,' said Lauren. 'An EMP will also knock out the guidance systems in a helicopter. They won't be able to fly here.'

'If that's the case, how are Lemski and his people planning to get off the island?' asked Jake.

'Simple,' said Lauren. 'They'll switch the disrupter off when they're ready to leave. My guess is they've already arranged for a helicopter to come down just after eleven o'clock. By then they'll either have the book, or they won't. Whatever's happened, they'll make their getaway.'

'Surely a helicopter won't have enough fuel to take them all the way to Russia,' pointed out Jake.

'It'll get them to the Finnish border,' said Stewart. 'Once they're there, they're safe.' He let out a heart-felt sigh. 'The trouble is, even if reinforcements do arrive, there's the issue of diplomatic immunity. When all this started up I was warned to tread very carefully. Softly-softly. Frankly, I was told to keep hands off. The powers that be don't want a difficult international incident.'

'But they've killed people! Surely that overrides any kind of diplomatic immunity!' protested Jake.

'We *think* they've killed people,' countered Stewart. 'We can't prove it.'

'Yes we can,' said Jake. 'We heard Muir admit to killing Dougie MacClain.'

'Ian Muir,' grunted Stewart. 'I had a hunch he was involved somewhere!'

'And we're your evidence against him!' insisted Jake.

'Muir is not a Russian,' said Stewart.

'He could be,' suggested Jake. 'Posing as an American.'

'Whatever he is, he's secure in that compound with the Russians, and we can't touch them.'

Jake looked enquiringly at Lauren.

'Then I guess it's up to us,' he said quietly.

'Yes,' said Lauren.

Stewart frowned.

'What do you mean?' he asked.

'We deliver the book to the Russians,' said Jake.

Chapter 26

'Oh no!' Stewart told them firmly. 'We've had enough deaths already on this island!'

'And there'll be two more unless we hand the book over,' said Jake. 'Rona and Alec.'

'You don't seriously believe they'll let them go, do you?' Stewart challenged them.

'They may,' said Lauren. 'It's a chance we have to take. If we don't, they'll die for certain. And, who knows, Lemski might even keep his word and let us all go.'

Stewart shook his head.

'You're being naive,' he said. 'You've just told me that you're the evidence that they were behind the death of Dougie MacClain. Which means they also killed John Gordon. They have to kill you to shut you up.'

'Possibly,' admitted Jake. 'But we can't let Alec and Rona die. We have to do something. We've got just over an hour before the deadline. At the moment, with this EMP operating and this whole business about diplomatic immunity and international incidents stopping any kind of official intervention, we're the only chance Alec and Rona have.'

Stewart fell silent, thinking about it. Finally, reluctantly, he said, 'I suppose so. But we'll be your back-up. Me and Constable Frierson. I can handle a rifle. I've done the training course.' He turned to Frierson. 'How about you, Constable?'

Frierson nodded.

'I'm not officially qualified, but I shot rabbits for the table when I was younger.'

'Good enough,' said Stewart. 'We'll both be there, ready to fire if things go wrong.'

'From a distance,' said Jake. 'If Lemski spots you, he might kill Alec and Rona straight away.'

'Of course from a distance,' snapped Stewart.

'How good are you with a rifle, Sergeant?' Jake asked.

'I don't like to boast, but I did well on the police range. Top score.'

'Could you disable a helicopter? Shoot out the rear rotor or something?'

Stewart frowned thoughtfully.

'Possibly,' he said.

'OK,' said Jake. 'Here's the plan. We go and carry

out the exchange and get Alec and Rona free. If Lauren's right, a helicopter will be landing immediately after, once they've switched off the EMP machine.'

'Who's Lauren?' asked Stewart sharply.

'I am,' said Lauren.

'So . . .' began Stewart, growling.

'Can we talk about that later?' pressed Jake. 'My guess is they plan to take us with them on the chopper.'

'Not necessarily,' said Lauren. 'They might plan to use us as guinea pigs again. Inject that stuff into us.'

And she shuddered at the memory of the hypodermic syringe, and seeing the Russian burst into flames.

'I doubt it,' said Jake. 'I reckon they'll keep that for later. Right now the main priority for Lemski is to get off this island.'

'They might just kill you,' said Stewart.

Jake shook his head.

'My hope is they'll take us as hostages,' he said. 'To make sure their helicopter is given free passage and not shot down mid-flight.'

'So you end up spending the rest of your lives in captivity in Russia?' asked Stewart.

'Or they kill us during the flight and throw us out somewhere over the North Sea, weighted down so our bodies don't come back to the surface,' said Lauren. 'All evidence neatly vanished.'

'Whichever, it's important that helicopter doesn't

leave the ground,' said Jake. 'It'll give time for your reinforcements to arrive. And we can get the book back.'

'I've already told you, we've got a diplomatic situation here,' Stewart reminded them. 'We can't charge in and arrest them.'

'No, but you can free us,' said Lauren.

'And if they start firing, surely you're allowed to fire back,' added Jake.

Stewart fell silent.

'OK,' he said. 'It's a plan.' He looked at his watch. 'It's just gone ten. We've got less than an hour. We need to get you kitted up.'

'Kitted up?' echoed Jake, puzzled.

'Just in case they change their mind and shoot you while you're standing here, waiting for the exchange to happen,' explained Stewart. 'Have we got any Kevlar body armour?' he asked Frierson.

'Just two jackets,' said Frierson.

'OK, then that's what you two will be wearing,' Stewart told Jake and Lauren. 'Wear them under your own clothes. It won't stop a head shot, or if they shoot you in the arms or legs, but it'll protect you if they go for the heart or chest. And most of these snipers do. It's a bigger target, easier to make sure of hitting. After all, they missed when they tried shooting you in the head.'

199

'I suppose that's a comfort,' admitted Lauren. 'But not much of one.'

'I've got another way to stop them shooting at us!' said Jake, as an idea struck him.

The others looked at him, quizzically.

'How?' asked Stewart.

'It's a long shot, but I thought we'd try fighting fire with fire,' said Jake. He forced what he hoped was a confident smile. 'Can you get your hands on a metal bucket and an asbestos glove?'

Chapter 27

Jake and Lauren rounded the small hillock and stopped. Directly in front of them, about a hundred metres away, was the cottage which Lemski and his Russians had now turned into a fortress. Jake could see the barrels of rifles poking out of the upstairs windows. The windows, however, hadn't been boarded up. Lemski wasn't expecting a long siege. Jake looked at his watch. Five minutes to eleven.

Jake looked down at the metal bucket he held in his asbestos-gloved right hand. Two pieces of coal at the bottom of it glowed red, sending smoke spiralling up. Not enough hot coal to make the bucket too hot to handle, but enough to produce smoke that could be seen from the cottage. In his left hand, Jake clutched the ancient book, the cause of all this death and mayhem. The Kevlar body armour felt bulky, as if he was wearing a life jacket beneath his coat.

'Stay here,' Jake whispered to Lauren.

'Lemski said he wanted us both.'

'It'll buy us some time if you don't come out at once,' said Jake. 'It's the book he's really after.'

Secretly, he was planning on leaving Lauren out of this; out of the final exchange. Leave her here, behind the protection of the small grassy hillock with DS Stewart and PC Frierson. He looked back at the two police officers, crouched down in the ditch-like area behind the long earth mound.

'If they start shooting, drop to the ground and lie flat,' Stewart instructed. 'I'll fire back and I don't want to shoot you.'

Jake nodded.

He looked towards the cottage. His mouth felt dry.

'I'm coming with you,' said Lauren.

'Please, Lauren, wait here at first,' pleaded Jake. Without turning round, he appealed to Stewart: 'Tell her.'

'He's right,' came Stewart's voice from the police officer's hiding place. 'Let's see if we can get away with just one of you going in. If we can mount a rescue, it'll make that rescue easier.'

Lauren hesitated, then nodded.

'I'm not going to let them kill you,' she whispered to Jake fiercely. 'Or take you to Russia.'

'I hope they don't,' said Jake, forcing a grin and

202

doing his best to put on an air of bravado. 'We've still got a lot of catching up to do.'

Jake took a deep breath, then moved forward along the track towards the wall that fronted the cottage. As he did so, he saw the rifle barrels at the upper windows move; and he stopped.

'Professor Lemski!' he called. 'I have the book!' And Jake brandished the book in the air. Then he moved the book so that it was directly above the metal bucket. 'If you look carefully, you will see smoke coming from this bucket I'm holding. That's because there are red hot coals in it! If you shoot me, the book will drop from my hand into the bucket and burn! It'll be turned to ashes before you can reach it! Release the MacClains first, and I'll hand it over to you.'

For a moment there was silence from the cottage, and then the distorted amplified voice of Lemski was heard calling back. He's using an old-fashioned megaphone, realised Jake.

'Very clever, Mr Wells! But we have no intention of shooting you! As I said in the message I left, all we want is the book back, and we will release the MacClains!'

'That's what you said, but do you really think I would trust you after all that's happened? You asked me to bring the book. Here it is. Now release the MacClains!'

There was another pause, then Lemski's distorted

mechanised voice called out, 'How do we know you'll keep your part of the bargain?'

'Because if I don't, I know you'll shoot me dead.'

There was a further pause, then Lemski called out: 'You will remain standing where you are, where we can see you!'

And where your sniper has got a clear shot at me, thought Jake.

'We will release the MacClains. They will be coming out accompanied by some of my people. They will be armed. You will remain standing where you are until the MacClains have gone past you. If you attempt to move from that spot, we will shoot you and the MacClains. My men are expert shots. They will not miss.'

'Don't worry, I'll stay here!' Jake shouted back.

'And we want to see Ms Graham standing next to you!' called Lemski.

'No!' called back Jake.

'Yes,' said Lauren's voice. Jake swung round and saw that Lauren had joined him.

'Go away!' he hissed.

'No,' she said. 'We're in this together. I'm not leaving without you.'

'They're going to kill me!' Jake told her angrily.

Lauren forced a smile.

'Then they might as well kill both of us,' she said.

204

The sound of the front door of the cottage opening made them both turn their attention in that direction. Alec and Rona stepped forward, slowly, their hands on top of their heads. Behind them came three men holding automatic rifles. As Alec and Rona moved slowly forward, the three men made sure they kept behind the pair, using the MacClains as human shields. The party of five, with the MacClains at the front, came nearer and nearer. The men held their guns trained directly on Jake and Lauren the whole time. Finally, when they were about twenty metres away from Jake and Lauren, the three men stopped and let Alec and Rona walk on, still with their hands clasped on the tops of their heads.

'Reckon we can make a run for it?' asked Lauren.

'Not with them that close,' said Jake. 'As soon as we turn to run, they'll shoot us. And, if they want to keep us alive to act as their hostages, they'll shoot us in the legs.'

'Pity we haven't got body armour leggings too,' muttered Lauren.

Alec and Rona drew level with them. Jake could see the strain etched on both their faces.

'Thank you,' whispered Alec.

'Later,' said Jake.

'Robbie and your wife are at Dr Patel's,' said Lauren.

'Is he OK?'

'He was hurt, but he's in safe hands,' said Lauren.

'Keep moving!' came Lemski's shout from the cottage.

Alec and Rona walked on, passing Jake and Lauren.

'Now, Mr Wells, bring the book to me!' called Lemski. 'You too, Ms Graham!'

'Not until the MacClains are out of the way!' called back Jake,

'You are wasting time!' snapped Lemski impatiently.

'I'm making sure our bargain is kept!' Jake called back.

He turned, and saw that Alec and Rona had speeded up, and had now taken refuge behind a rocky outcrop.

'Time to go,' said Jake.

He was just about to move forward, when there was the sound of a metallic click from behind the mound of earth where DS Stewart and PC Frierson were hiding. At once, one of the Russians turned and fired a burst from his automatic rifle into that direction, which ripped into and through the earth. There was a gurgling moan from behind the hillock, and then a deadly silence.

Jake and Lauren exchanged horrified, sickened looks. Stewart and Frierson were dead. Their back-up had gone.

Chapter 28

'Put the bucket down on the ground, Mr Wells! Slowly! Or you will be next!'

Lemski's voice rang out, echoing across the heath.

Jake put the metal bucket down.

'Now walk towards my men!'

Jake looked at Lauren and gave her a rueful smile.

'You should have stayed out of this. Now I'm going to have to rescue you all over again,' he told her.

'Move now!' called Lemski, his voice more urgent this time. 'And keep your hands in the air where we can see them! And hold the book up high the whole time!'

Jake and Lauren moved forward, hands and the book in the air. They reached the three armed Russians. One Russian grabbed Jake by the arm, while another took hold of Lauren's shoulder. Then they hurried them towards the cottage while the third followed them at speed, moving backwards, rifle sweeping from side to side, ready to fire.

Once inside the cottage, the door slammed shut and was locked. Jake and Lauren found themselves face to face with Muir, who held a pistol and glowered at them.

'You put us to a lot of trouble!' he snarled.

'But that trouble is over now, Mr Muir,' said Lemski as he appeared from the stairs.

He walked over to Jake and took the book from his hand; then opened it to make sure Jake had brought the real book with him.

'Excellent!' he said. 'We can leave.' He turned to Muir and added: 'We'll take them with us in the first helicopter.'

The *first* helicopter, thought Jake. He looked around at the people in the room. Of course, it would need more than one to evacuate this lot. So even if Stewart had stayed alive long enough to take out the helicopter, there would be others on their way.

'Look, you've got the book,' said Jake. 'You might as well let us go.'

'So you can go telling tales about us?' snorted Muir. 'No chance!'

'Also, it's less likely that our transport will be shot down if they know you're with us,' said Lemski.

So we were right, thought Jake. We're going to be hostages.

Lemski called something in Russian, and one of the men went to a machine on a table at one side of the room and pressed a switch on it. Immediately, a vague humming sound that Jake had been aware of from the moment they entered the cottage stopped.

'The EMP generator,' said Lauren.

Lemski smiled.

'Well done, Ms Graham.' He beamed. 'You will be a great benefit to us when we return to Russia. You have knowledge, and creative intelligence. A formidable combination.' He turned to Jake, and his smile faded. 'You, Mr Wells, have persistence. I'm not sure if that will be of any use. We shall have to see when we get back.' He barked a command in Russian, and one of the men picked up a radio communicator and said something tersely into it.

'He's calling in the helicopter,' Lauren told Jake.

'And you speak Russian as well!' chuckled Lemski.

'No,' said Lauren. 'But it was the obvious next move once the EMP generator's been switched off, and before the British authorities can react.'

'The British authorities!' sneered Lemski. 'Amateurs!'

In the distance they heard the sound of a helicopter. Jake frowned.

You must have had that stashed somewhere pretty close,' he commented.

'On a container ship not too far away.' Lemski smiled. 'This has been well-planned for some time.'

'Not that well planned,' said Jake, 'otherwise you wouldn't have needed to kill so many people.'

Lemski's face clouded over and he scowled in the direction of Muir. 'Sometimes things do not always go as planned,' he snapped.

Muir shrugged.

'Hey, I'm a guy who gets things done,' he said. 'I moved things forward and saved your ass. Don't forget that.'

Lemski didn't reply. Instead, he gestured towards the door.

'It's time to go,' he said.

He said something in Russian, and one of the armed men went to the door and opened it, then stepped out, gun poised and ready to fire. He checked the situation outside was clear, then he nodded to Lemski.

Lemski tucked the precious book into an inner pocket and produced a pistol, which he pointed at Jake and Lauren.

'You will go out with us and get aboard the helicopter. If you attempt to run, we will shoot you and haul you on board. Your journey will then be very painful indeed.'

The sound of the helicopter was much louder now, the noise of its engine deafening.

Prodded by the pistols of Lemski and Muir, Jake and Lauren stepped out of the cottage. The helicopter was hovering just outside the courtyard. As Jake watched, it came down and settled.

'Right! Move!' snapped Lemski.

'And keep your heads low!' added Muir.

They hurried towards the helicopter, crouching low. Although the main rotor had stopped spinning, Jake noticed that the smaller rear rotor was still going round, and he made sure to keep well clear of it as they reached the chopper.

There were five seats inside the helicopter: one next to the pilot, two behind the front seats, and a third at the back. Muir climbed into the machine and took the seat next to the pilot, then kept his pistol trained on Jake and Lauren as they climbed aboard. Muir gestured at the two seats in the middle of the craft.

'Strap yourselves in tight, and don't try any funny business,' he warned.

Jake and Lauren sat down and began to fasten their seat belts. Lemski climbed aboard and took the seat behind them. He still kept his pistol aimed at them. He snapped an order in Russian, and the pilot engaged the rotor. They felt the helicopter shake, and then begin to rise.

They were going to Russia; and a sick feeling filled Jake as he realised that they'd never ever get back.

Chapter 29

Suddenly the helicopter gave a violent lurch, throwing them all around. Jake and Lauren, their seat belts still not properly fastened, were hurled out of their seats; as were Lemski and Muir.

'What the?!' roared Muir.

He tried to stand up, but fell over again as the helicopter gave another dreadful lurch; and then came back to earth with a crash and nearly toppled over. At the impact, Lemski had fallen out through the open doorway and was lying on the ground.

'Jump!' yelled Jake.

And he grabbed Lauren and almost threw her out through the door, leaping down after her. They landed on the figure of Lemski, who yelled out in pain and writhed, making them both stumble. Jake saw the edge of the book sticking out of the professor's inside pocket. He reached down and snatched it up, but as he did so he felt a punch in his back, and then clawing fingers grab him round the neck.

Jake swung his elbow back, and heard a grunt of pain and angry swearing in English as the fingers released their grip. Muir!

Jake swung round, just as Muir leapt at him again. The American's gun had gone, possibly fallen under one of the seats, Jake guessed.

Jake swung a punch as hard as he could into the American's face and felt it connect, and an intense pain shot through his hand and up his arm.

I've broken my hand! realised Jake.

He saw Lauren getting to her feet and reaching into the helicopter, and guessed she was reaching for one of the guns. Muir was too intent on getting the book back from Jake to keep his eye on Lauren.

I need to get him away from her, thought Jake. It's the book he's after!

As the American once again threw himself at Jake, Jake brought his elbow up into Muir's face, sending him staggering back. Then he broke into a run, clutching the book in his one good hand, but before he could get far the American was on him again, crashing into Jake's back and sending them both smashing to the ground.

Jake twisted round and kicked out, and felt his shoe thud into Muir; but the American was crazed, nothing

213

seemed to affect him. Jake kicked again, and this time he felt Muir's hold on him relax enough for Jake to scramble up and run. As Jake did, he realised that the helicopter had come down nearer to the edge of the cliff, and that edge was now just a metre away from him.

Jake pulled to a halt and turned, just in time to see Muir rushing towards him, arms outstretched, an expression of fury on his face. Jake swung the book out, as if he was going to hurl it over the edge of the cliff, and Muir launched himself in desperation at Jake, his fingers clutching for the book. As Muir's hands closed on it, Jake snatched it back and then kicked out, his foot hitting Muir on the side of the knee. Muir yelled in pain and stumbled. Jake saw the American scrabbling at the air, desperately trying to regain his balance . . . and then he fell, disappearing over the edge of the cliff with a scream.

Jake moved back from the edge and saw Lauren engaged in a struggle with four of the Russians, who'd obviously rushed out of the cottage when the helicopter came down. She had the pistol in her hand and was trying to aim it, but the weight of numbers was overwhelming her, and she went down, taking the Russians with her.

Jake ran towards her, and as he did he saw Lemski lurch to his feet. The Russian professor had managed to get his hands on a pistol, and Jake saw that he was trying to get an aim on Lauren.

'No!' yelled Jake.

At the shout Lemski swung round, and now he pointed the pistol at Jake.

BANG!!

The bullet hit Jake right in the middle of the chest, knocking him over backwards. Even with the protection of the body armour, the impact hurt.

As he struggled to his knees, he saw Lemski approaching, the pistol held out at arm's length, pointing straight at Jake.

'Give me the book!' roared the professor.

'No!' shouted back Jake.

This time, the professor swung the pistol back and then brought it down hard on the side of Jake's head. Pain flooded through Jake's skull. Then he felt more pain as the gun was smashed down on his good hand that held the book, and the book dropped from his fingers.

Lemski snatched up the book, and then hit Jake with the gun one more time, the metal barrel crashing agonisingly against his skull and sending him face first down to the ground.

He lay there, dazed and in pain. He struggled to push himself up off the ground. I have to get up, he thought. I have to save Lauren! I mustn't let them take her!

He heard the sound of an approaching helicopter. The second helicopter. This one would take Lemski, and Lauren, and the book, off the island. If that happened, he'd never see Lauren again.

He forced himself to stand up. Both his hands were nothing but pain; the fingers of both hands were broken. But I'll stop them some way, vowed Jake as he forced himself to run towards where Lauren was now being hauled to her feet by the Russians. He saw Lemski turn and point the gun at him. Because of the deafening noise of the helicopter now immediately overhead, he never heard the pistol go off; he just saw the puff of smoke from the barrel of the pistol, and then that powerful impact again as the bullet struck him, smashing him backwards to the earth once more.

Dazed, he lay on the ground and saw the dark shape of the helicopter, this one bigger than the last. And then he heard gunfire . . .

Chapter 30

The gunfire stopped abruptly. What had happened?

Jake pulled himself up from the ground and was stunned to see the Russians, including Professor Lemski, standing with their hands in the air. Lauren was there, as well, also with her hands above her head. Facing them were a group of men clad completely in black from head to foot, all wearing black helmets with black visors, and training automatic rifles on the Russians and Lauren.

Special forces! realised Jake. They're ours!

'Hey!' called Jake, pointing towards Lauren. 'She's one of ours!'

Immediately, one of the black-clad soldiers ran over to Jake, his gun pointing at him.

'Hands on your head!' he snapped, his voice coming through a speaker system, giving it a mechanical, almost cybernetic tone.

'I'm on your side!' protested Jake.

'Hands on your head!' repeated the soldier, firmer this time.

Jake groaned and raised his hands to the top of his head.

'That's the best I can do,' he said. 'My fingers are broken.'

Jake sat in Dr Patel's surgery as the doctor tended to his fingers, gently wrapping a long gauze bandage around them.

'Only four of your fingers are broken,' Dr Patel told him. 'Unfortunately, it's two on each hand.'

'That's all right,' said Lauren from the couch where she was observing. 'I can fetch and carry for him.'

'I won't be able to hold a knife and fork to eat,' complained Jake.

'I'm sure you'll find a way round that,' said Lauren.

The door opened and DS Stewart came in.

'How's he doing, Doc?' he asked.

'He's fine,' said Dr Patel.

'I'm not fine!' exclaimed Jake. 'I've got four broken fingers!'

'It could have been a lot worse,' said Stewart. 'How long will it take?'

'This is the last one,' said Dr Patel. 'Twenty minutes.'

'OK. When you're ready, Mr Wells, there's someone

who wants to talk to you at the station via our Skype system.'

'Who?' asked Jake.

'He didn't give his name. He said you'd know who he was.'

Of course, thought Jake. Gareth Findlay-Weston. His boss at the Department of Science, and head of an MI5 section. Or, rather, his *former* boss. Although, according to the piece of paper that Gareth had sent to Pam Gordon, Jake had been reinstated. Was Gareth calling to renege on that? More importantly, was he going to renege on allowing Lauren permission to return to the UK?

Stewart drove them to the police station, Lauren in the front passenger seat, and Jake in the back, his plaster-encased hands cradled on his lap.

'We thought you were dead,' said Jake. 'You and PC Frierson. We heard you groan when they shot you.'

'The bullets hit the earth bank, which acted like a sandbag. I let out a groan to make them think they'd got us. I was hoping they'd then just go away.'

'And if they hadn't?' asked Lauren.

'I suppose I'd have had to shoot them,' said Stewart. 'But it wouldn't have changed things much. We'd have still had a siege situation on the island. And there was a danger of both of you getting killed in the crossfire.'

'How did those special forces guys know when and where to come down?' asked Jake.

'You tell me,' said Stewart. 'You're the spooks.'

'We're not spooks,' protested Jake. 'We're just innocent people caught up in this.'

'Innocent people don't get MI5 ordering the police to back off from them,' countered Stewart.

'What's happened to Professor Lemski and the rest of his Russians?'

'You'd better ask your chief spook,' said Stewart. 'All I know is that the special forces guys took them all away. Right now, I know nothing. But I'm sure I'll be getting orders from on high shortly telling me what I can and can't tell the media.'

'OK, what about things you can tell us?' asked Lauren. 'How's Robbie?'

'He's OK,' said Stewart. 'He's been taken to the mainland to be treated, but there are no serious internal injuries. And Dr Patel did a good job patching him up temporarily.'

'Pam Gordon?'

'Also good, according to the medicos. In fact, the only fatality out of today's chaos was your friend, Ian Muir. That dive he took over the cliff killed him. He broke his neck.'

'Justice in a way,' murmured Lauren. 'He died the same way he killed Dougie MacClain.'

'Not quite,' said Stewart. 'Muir killed Dougie and then threw his body off the cliff.' He looked at Jake quizzically in the rear-view mirror. 'Unless you're telling me that you killed Muir, Mr Wells?'

'Absolutely not!' said Jake firmly. 'It was an accident. We fought, and he tripped and fell over the cliff.'

'Of course he did,' said Stewart with a hint of sarcasm. 'I guess accidents happen a lot around you spooks.'

'We're not spooks!' Jake repeated impatiently.

'Of course you're not,' said Stewart. He slowed the car as they approached the small police station. 'And now you can talk to the man who's not your secret boss.'

Jake and Lauren sat side by side on hard wooden chairs in the office at the back of the police station. On the desk in front of them was an open laptop, and on the screen the face of Gareth Findlay-Weston beamed at them. Smiling, as always, thought Jake. That same smile he'd be wearing whether he was about to praise someone or execute them.

'I hear you two have had quite an eventful time on Mull,' said Gareth. 'But then I always find the Hebrides very invigorating. The air in particular is very bracing.'

'I have the document you signed,' said Jake.

'Which document would that be?' asked Gareth.

'The one you sent to Pam Gordon, giving permission for Lauren to return to the UK, and me to get my job back.'

Gareth frowned.

'Sounds like a forgery to me,' he said. 'I can hardly imagine anyone in my position would authorise such a document, unless under extreme pressure, possibly blackmail. And, as I'm sure you know, any document obtained under blackmail is not valid in a court of law.'

'Now look!' exploded Jake angrily, and he shook his bandaged fists at the webcam.

'Calm down, Jake,' said Gareth. 'You might do further damage to those poor hands of yours.' Then he smiled. 'Anyway, you can rest assured, that document will be honoured.'

Jake's expression changed from fury, to stunned astonishment.

'It will?' he asked.

'Of course,' said Gareth. 'I value you highly as a worker, Jake, as you know. Also, to be frank, keeping a close watch on the pair of you is an expense this department can do without, especially in these difficult economic times. It will be far cheaper to have you both where we can keep an eye on you. So, yes, Ms Graham; you may remain in this country. And Jake, I expect you to return to work once your injuries have healed.'

Jake wanted to yell out in joy, give an exultant cry of 'Yess!', but he did his best to contain himself. Instead, he looked at Lauren and gave her the broadest smile possible, and she smiled back, her eyes sparkling.

But that was for later. Right now, there were still many questions that Jake wanted answers to.

'Why did you send in the SAS?' he asked. 'Considering what Pam Gordon had said about the Russians and diplomatic immunity.'

A look of displeasure crossed Gareth's face.

'I do wish you wouldn't throw people's names around in a public conversation,' he rebuked Jake.

'I'm sorry,' said Jake. 'I thought this was a private conversation.'

'Don't be silly, Jake. There are no such things as private conversations any more, not where modern technology is concerned. Anyway, to answer your question. First, the SAS were not sent in.'

Jake frowned, puzzled.

'If they weren't the SAS, who were they?' he asked. 'They acted like them.'

'Let us just say they were experts in their job,' said Gareth. 'Which is dealing with dangerous hostage situations.'

'Which is what the SAS do,' insisted Jake.

Again, Gareth gave them a look of irritation.

'At the moment I am feeling benevolent towards

223

you,' he said. 'My attitude may change if you continue to annoy me.'

Lauren gave Jake a sharp and painful nudge in the thigh with her finger that meant: *Shut up. We've got what we want. If you upset him, he might take it back.*

'I'm sorry,' said Jake. 'I won't interrupt any more.'

'Good,' said Gareth. 'As it turns out, the professor was not acting in any official capacity. The so-called archaeological dig was his own enterprise.'

Lies, thought Jake. No one could carry out an undertaking like Professor Lemski's dig without some sort of official government backing. However, his thigh still hurt from where Lauren had just jabbed him. Keep your mouth shut, he told himself. Don't make waves.

'The Russian government did initially approve his excavations, which is why the issue of diplomatic immunity arose,' continued Gareth, 'but once he became too extreme in his actions, they withdrew their diplomatic immunity from him and his team. They distanced themselves from him completely, describing him as a "rogue activist", and nothing to do with the Russian government.'

'Do we believe them?'

Gareth shrugged.

'Whether we do or not is irrelevant. What matters is that there will be no repercussions between our two governments over what happened. Professor Lemski was acting completely on his own. And, of course, he has been handed back to the Russian authorities, along with the rest of his team.'

'So he gets away with it. With killing Dougie MacClain and John Gordon.'

'We don't believe the professor was actually involved in their deaths. It seems that may well have been Muir, acting on his own initiative.'

'But Muir worked for Lemski!'

'We don't know that for sure. Whether he started out as an independent operator who linked up with Lemski; or whether he was in place beforehand, we don't know. We're still trying to find out more about him. Of course, now he's dead, much of that will be academic. In fact, with his death, I think we can say, "Case closed".'

'What about the book?' asked Lauren.

'Ah yes, the book.' Gareth smiled. 'That would appear to have come into our possession.'

'Those soldiers took it off me!' said Jake.

'Standard procedure when dealing with a hostage situation, to check all persons — including the hostages — for hidden weapons, or anything that might pose a threat.'

'It was a book!' said Jake.

'A *dangerous* book,' said Gareth. He looked at his watch. 'Actually, I have another conference call about

225

to start. So we shall say goodbye. Welcome back to the United Kingdom, Ms Graham. I'm sure you will be able to sort things out with your friends in New Zealand. As for you, Jake, I look forward to hearing from you when the doctor certifies you fit to return to work.'

And with that, the image of Gareth on the screen was replaced by a black square, and the message: *Contact terminated* appeared.

Jake turned to Lauren and sighed.

'We lost the book,' he said.

'But we got each other back,' said Lauren. 'And there'll be other books.'

He leant forward and kissed her.

'Yes,' he said. 'There'll be other books.'

Chapter 31

Robbie lay propped up against the pillows in his hospital bed, a drip attached to his arm. He gave Jake and Lauren a glum look.

'We lost the book,' he said.

'But they saved your life,' said Rona.

Jake and Lauren both knew they couldn't leave the area without visiting Robbie in the hospital at Oban. Rona had gone to stay with one of her many aunts on the mainland so she could visit Robbie every day.

'I know,' said Robbie, 'and I'm grateful for that, I really am. But we're Watchers. Our job was to protect the book.'

'You couldn't stop it being found,' Lauren said. 'Lemski knew where it was, and he had unlimited resources at his disposal. And weapons, and people who would use them. Your Uncle Dougie tried, and look what happened to him.'

'I suppose you're right,' said Robbie. But his down-cast expression showed he didn't really feel it.

'But it's in a safe place,' said Rona. 'Isn't that right?' she said to Lauren and Jake.

'Oh yes,' Jake assured them. 'It's locked securely away where no one can get at it.' Not even us, he reflected ruefully.

'How long do they think you'll have to stay in hospital?' Lauren asked Robbie.

'The doctor said I should be able to leave tomorrow. Luckily, the bullet didn't hit anything serious. And Dr Patel did a great job, which helped.'

'Excellent,' said Jake. He looked at his watch, and then said apologetically, 'Actually, we'd better make a move. We've got to get back to Glasgow and catch a train.'

'Mum and Dad say you're always welcome at Craigmount,' said Rona. 'As friends, not paying guests.' She gave them both a shy smile. 'We hope you'll come back.'

'I'm sure we will,' said Jake.

'We certainly will,' added Lauren firmly. 'And next time we'll enjoy the island, without being chased over it by people with guns.'

'And stuff that sets you on fire,' said Robbie.

'About that, what will happen to Professor Lemski?' asked Rona. 'I mean, the experiment is out there, in the open. Will he develop it?'

'That depends on what happens to him now he's back in Russia,' said Jake. 'I mean, he could be locked up.'

'I doubt it,' said Lauren. 'People like the professor are too important to their governments to be kept out of things. And too dangerous.'

Professor Lemski sat in the palatial office of the Minister of Science in Moscow and sipped at the glass of steaming tea.

'That was very nearly an extremely nasty diplomatic incident, Fyodor,' commented the minister, a large man with a bald head and startlingly bushy eyebrows.

'It was the American's fault,' countered Lemski. 'Muir.'

'But the operation was under your control.'

'My people were under my control,' corrected Lemski. 'Muir was a loose cannon. A maverick. I warned against using him from the very start.'

'Yes yes,' said the minister hastily. 'But the book is lost.'

'The book may be, but not all the information it contained,' said Lemski.

'You photocopied it?' asked the minister, leaning forward expectantly. Then his eager expression vanished, as he remembered: 'But the British took all your papers before they released you.'

'They did,' said Lemski. He tapped his forehead. 'But you forget, I have a photographic memory.'

'Excellent!' said the minister. 'So the experiments can continue!'

'The experiments are done,' said Lemski 'We know the constituents of the serum, and their proportions. I propose we move on to the next project.' He leant forward. 'There are many more books from the Malichea library hidden. Not just in the Highlands and islands of Scotland from the abbey at Iona, but from the library at Glastonbury. We need to find them, and to do that we need to find The Index!'

The minister frowned, a doubtful expression on his face.

'There are many people searching for them,' he pointed out. 'We can come to some kind of civilised arrangement with most of them. Even some of the more — ah — dubious organisations. But what about this English couple? You mentioned the problems that Mr Muir caused us because he was a maverick. As I understand it, this Mr Wells and Ms Graham could be even worse.'

Lemski nodded.

'Yes, I agree,' he said. 'I am convinced that as a result I shall meet them again.' A nasty smile lit up his face. 'And when I do, I will have my revenge on them for what happened on Mull. I will destroy them, piece by piece!' His smile broadened, and he raised his glass of tea in a toast. 'To revenge!'

Want to know what happens next?
Read on for a gripping taster of
THE LAST ENEMY . . .

Prologue

Alex Munro, CEO of Pierce Randall, got out of his chauffeur-driven car and looked along Crouch End Broadway, his eye lighting on the Red Hen café just five paces away from where he stood. It was very rare that a man in his position, one of the most powerful lawyers in the world, made a 'home visit'. People came to see *him*, not the other way round. But this was a special case. The person he'd come here to meet could well be the way into the mother lode — the key to the whole hidden library of the Order of Malichea. If it turned out to be so, then this could signal millions — no, *billions* of dollars coming into the company.

His driver, Gerald, closed the rear passenger door and shot Munro a questioning look that asked: *Do you need me with you?* Munro shook his head. No, he didn't need Gerald with him, everything seemed safe. His security people had checked the café out — the owners, the clientele. Five of his bodyguards, all ex-military, were inside posing as customers and ready to spring into action if needed. If there was any hint of trouble, they'd have sorted it out before Munro even entered the place.

He looked at his watch and checked it against the giant clock on the imposing brick monument in the centre of the Broadway. Two p.m. That was the time agreed. He wondered if the person he was due to meet was already inside the café, waiting for him, or whether they'd be late. He hoped they'd be on time; he couldn't stand unpunctuality.

He nodded at Gerald, who got back into the car. Then Munro moved across the pavement towards the café.

He never made it.

As he took his second step, the bullet smashed into the back of his head and ripped through his brain, sending blood erupting out from the exit wound. He was dead before he hit the ground.

The figure high up on the roof of the old building overlooking the Broadway began to take apart the sniper rifle and put it into its case. When he reappeared on the street below in a few moments, he would just be carrying an ordinary attaché case. He'd disappear into the crowd, just another passer-by going about his business.

The first part of the plan had been carried out. Alex Munro was dead. Now to concentrate on his next target: Jake Wells.